RESEARCHED DEATH

G.L. BARBOUR

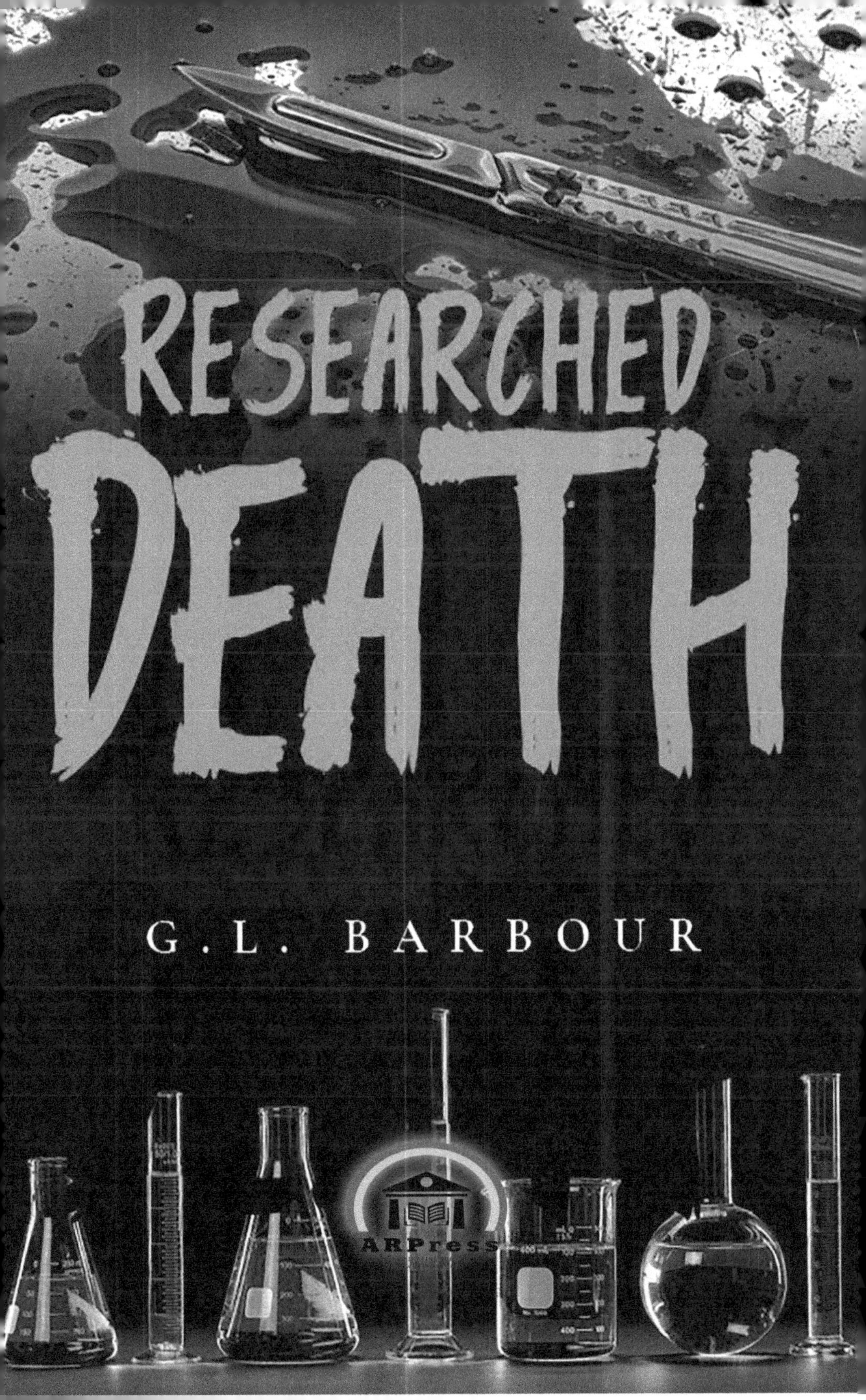

RESEARCHED DEATH

G. L. BARBOUR

ARPress
45 Dan Road Suite 5
Canton MA 02021

Hotline: 1(888) 821-0229
Fax: 1(508) 545-7580

Ordering Information:
Quantity sales. Special discounts are available on quantity purchases by corporations, associations, and others. For details, contact the publisher at the address above.

Printed in the United States of America.

ISBN-13:	Paperback	979-8-89356-521-8
	eBook	979-8-89356-523-2
	Hardback	979-8-89356-522-5

Library of Congress Control Number: 2024902553

Other Books by G. L. Barbour

<u>Academic</u>

Quality in the Veterans Health Administration
Redefining a Public Health System

<u>Fiction</u>

The Ron Looney Series

Death Unexpected
One, Two, Three Times a Murder
A Twisted Death
Naked Death
Alibi for Death

<u>Other</u>

Montana in the Rearview Mirror

Contents

PROLOGUE

Sunset and dusk had come and passed into the growing gray of the evening. The edges of the building were not as sharp as an hour before. A brisk breeze from the northwest carried a slight chill and made the early spring air feel lighter than usual. Sounds of the city were audible but muted in the dream-like conditions. The parking area was poorly lit and contained only a few scattered vehicles.

A man exiting the building gently broke the quiet atmosphere. The man seemed tired, his steps were slow, and he did not raise his head as if he were watching every step. He raised his head once, at the top of the stairs to locate his car. He appeared to trudge more slowly as he approached the vehicle. He was wearing blue scrubs and Velcro closured athletic shoes. The scrubs were wrinkled and partially covered by a short sport jacket. When he reached the vehicle, he pulled his keys from his jacket pocket, opened the door, and plopped down heavily on the driver's seat.

He sat quietly for a moment then, after a deep sigh, he pulled the door closed, leaned forward, and started the car. But, instead of driving off, he put both hands atop the steering wheel and leaned his head on his hands and remained in that position for several seconds.

Finally, he sat up and let out another sigh, and leaned back in his seat. He was briefly aware of movement in the rear seat before a noose of some material was quickly placed over his head, shoved down to his throat, and pulled tight around his neck. His hands immediately went to his neck and discovered it was caught in a heavy leather belt. The belt was drawn tight and he found he could not move forward; before he could make a serious attempt at fighting the snare, he heard a somewhat familiar voice whispering harshly in his right ear.

"Calm down. Don't make sudden moves."

The man in the driver's seat was able to squeak out a minimal response. He pointed at the belt and it was loosened a fraction.

"What you want?" the driver whispered back.

"Later. Don't talk. I have this belt where I can cut off all air and blood flow in less than a second. It's around the headrest support. If you make any attempt to signal someone for help, I'll pull it tight. Do you understand?"

The driver tried to nod assent but found his head movement restricted. He looked up in an attempt to see his attacker in the rearview mirror but found it turned upward and of no use.

"We're going to take a little ride."

"Where?" came the gasping question.

"Never mind. I'll direct you," the whisperer responded. "Turn right out of the parking area. Go right at the next light,"

CHAPTER 1

Physicians and residents were filing into the small auditorium for the Saturday morning research conference at New City Hospital in Cincinnati. These conferences were a blend of various scholarly endeavors and were usually fun while remaining routine. The conference occurred in a small auditorium that held only about 30 people. That was generally sufficient because the meeting was not mandatory, and only a couple dozen of the house officers and attendings regularly came to the conference. Tom Bolling, chief of staff at New City, had created the conference several years ago as a forum with two specific purposes. The first and major reason for the gathering was an opportunity for faculty and staff researchers scheduled to make a presentation at a national meeting the chance to do so in front of a friendly audience. Friendly, to the extent that presenters knew they wouldn't be heckled. And presenters could count on a bonus, as they expected to get constructive criticism of everything from their choice of words to the design of their PowerPoint slides. Tom knew that such preparation and critique would make the final presentations more professional and add luster to the academic program at New City and their Southwest Ohio Medical School affiliate.

Tom had a second reason for the conference. He wanted the venue to attract the young men and women in the various training programs to learn what research was going on in their teaching facility. He hoped the experience would tweak their interest and result in several of them getting involved in some of the activity themselves. So, Tom had organized the conference to involve two presentations each week, one a 10-minute talk in preparation for a national stage followed by fifteen or twenty minutes of feedback. The second presentation by a funded researcher was intended more toward explaining his or her work and goals and laboratory procedures. Over the years, several researchers had benefitted from this opportunity by obtaining ideas and assistance in solving conundrums in their program. Quite pleasing to Tom, more than a dozen residents had become involved in research activities because of their attendance at the Saturday research conference.

Tom Bolling was a retired U.S. Air Force General officer and orthopedic surgeon, recruited to New City several years previously. Two previous Chiefs of Staff had left the position because of difficulties marrying a clinical hospital staff with the activities and expectations of a teaching institution. New City was a very respected clinically-based institution, delivering solid quality of care for the community. Its affiliation with Southwest Ohio Medical School, also in Cincinnati, had experienced a turbulent period for the first several years. Tom was recruited and tasked with improving the integration of New City activity with the university goals of a strong teaching program. So far, Tom had some successes, but the daily resistance to an academic approach to delivering health care presented by the Hospital Director, Sam Mastone, was discouraging. Fortunately, The Director did not attend the Saturday morning conference, giving Tom a bit of a respite from explaining why certain aspects of care in a teaching hospital were different from a non-teaching one.

Tom had specifically pushed the Director of Research at New City, Dr. Alston MacFarlane, to publicize the event each week with bulletins around the facility announcing topics and presenters. Further, Tom himself made a pitch to the assembled residents about the opportunities for them in research. MacFarlane and Dr. Donald Piringa, chair of the Research Committee, repeatedly encouraged the funded researchers to find ways to involve the resident trainees in various aspects of their research projects. Generally, the process was becoming a pleasant ritual.

This particular morning, the long presentation belonged to a general surgeon, Adam Schlecter. He noted the clinical circumstance fueling his research is the need for long-term intravenous medications, mostly antibiotics, in patients who otherwise did not need hospitalization. The idea that such patients could be treated at home with a permanent intravenous access device conflicted with several ethical issues when the patient had, for instance, an infection in their heart valve because of their prior use of intravenous illegal drugs. Sending such patients home without scrutiny with an access device that would make their i.v. drug abuse easier is not condoned in the profession.

Schlecter briefly sketched the issue in an introduction and turned most of his time to explain his attempt to solve the issue. He had developed an artificial membrane from human collagen and plasma proteins that could be manipulated to be more or less porous to certain-sized molecules. Using some other clever techniques, Schlecter developed a method of creating a bubble of this membrane. His presentation centered on how he could craft bubbles of varying sizes and noted how they were soft and flexible, suitable for implantation.

His presentation then focused on what he was putting in the bubbles: one or more antibiotics. He went on to show that the active ingredients leach out of the bubble at highly reproducible rates in water-filled vats. He said these findings provided a basis for trying the use of the system in animals. He concluded his presentation with the early results of measuring blood levels of antibiotics in rabbits implanted with a bubble containing antibiotics. He noted the skewed results and mentioned some of the difficulties still facing this research.

In the discussion period that followed his presentation, Schlecter was questioned about the biggest barrier to his system. He replied,

"It's the lack of long-term coverage, I guess. The animal models show promise, but the bubbles only work for a day or so before the antibiotics are gone. We need to address the porosity to get longer diffusion times."

"Can you use higher concentrations of antibiotics and use a less porous membrane?" asked one of the oncologists.

"Possibly. We are going to try that in animals next."

"You know, Adam, it's possible we could use that delivery method for some chemotherapy drugs," the oncologist continued.

"It's quite possible we can adjust the porosity and arrange for slow delivery of many different agents," Schlecter said, "but presently, we need to move to larger animals so we can first try using larger bubbles. Thank you for your comments."

He received a nice round of applause.

As the applause faded, everyone began collecting their belongings to head for home. Tom waited for Schlecter at the door and walked with him back toward the research wing.

"You didn't seem as ebullient about your progress this morning as usual Adam, what's up?"

"I'm, ah, a little distracted, that's all. This work is going well. Slow but well. You know we spent the first half of our funding period just perfecting the membrane porosity function."

"You look tired, too. Everything else all right?"

"I've got a teenaged son who just finished high school and wants to do an 'off-year' before deciding if he wants to go to college. It's driving me nuts!"

"Tell him I suggested that he join the military."

"Oh, Alan would get a good laugh out of that suggestion."

"Look, the military will take a bright and capable 18-year-old and make a mature, bright, and seasoned 22-year-old adult out of him. Give him skills and training and the GI Bill."

"Yeah, I heard something about that. What's that do for him?"

"It will cover his costs of college; tuition and fees and a stipend for books plus a monthly housing allowance."

"Whoa, I didn't know that. Alan could take a few years and get free college."

"And in the meantime, he will likely get to see some of the world."

"He probably wouldn't like those parts where people shoot at you for being an American."

"Don't blame him. But there are lots more parts where he can see sights and eat amazing food and ..."

"Hold on, Tom. You don't have to sell me. Alan is the one without a goal or direction right now."

They had come to the place where the hallway forked, and Tom stopped walking. "Tell you what, if you can get him to come to see me, I'll do the sales pitch myself."

Schlecter made a wry grin. "Maybe. We'll see. First, I gotta get an interim report to Mac. It seems the NIH has overstretched its budget and is looking to cut back on some programs. So, they put more non-research tasks on those of us with grants."

"Will you be all right?"

"Don't know. I have to write up our current results in words and phrases that sound like Nobel laureate level work. It all depends on whether the reviewers can take a joke, you know."

Chapter 2

Thursday, October 8

Tom Bolling closely examined the cereal in his bowl as he leaned against the counter in his kitchen. He thought the nuts advertised on the cereal carton were definitely not as evident in the bowl as they were in the picture on the front of the box. As he frowned at this recognition, Sandra looked up from where she was eating a yogurt cup at the counter and asked, "Honey, is there a worm in your cereal?"

"No worm and very few pecans, either."

"The advertised value of that cereal is the addition of fiber to your diet for a beneficial effect on serum cholesterol."

"Are you reading from the box?"

"No. I remember all the ads. And I'm pretty certain there were no promises of 'plentiful pecans'.

"Look at the picture," Yom said, showing her box. "That's clearly false advertising. I expected far more nuts than what I'm getting."

"Maybe you should take over the shopping and see if you can find a more nutty cereal that's to your liking and up to your standards."

"No deal. My role is to observe and call any shortcomings to attention."

"That certainly was your role in the Air Force, general. Not so much here at home."

"My apologies to the CEO. I have clearly overstepped my bounds," he said with a wry smile as he took the last spoonful of cereal.

"Apology accepted. Further, to indicate that I heard the 'observation', I will request that the CSO obtain additional pecans for addition to the cereal."

"The CSO?"

"You know, the Chief Shopping Officer."

"Oh, right." Tom moved to the sink and rinsed his bowl and spoon before adding them to the open dishwasher. "Of Course, the pecan allocation is only one of the things I have to worry about. And I'd really like a Chief Something Officer to help with things at the hospital."

"What's the big worry this week?"

"Well, even if Sam is staying in his lane, there's always something a bit awry," he replied, standing behind her and putting his hands on her shoulders. "This past week, I've gotten more and more worried bout Adam Schlecter."

"The surgeon? With the wife that looks older than him?"

"That is not the way he is referred to in the hospital," Tom smiled as he kissed Sandra's hair and moved toward the doorway. "But yes, the surgeon."

"What's wrong with him?" Sandra asked, throwing her yogurt cup in the trash and turning toward him.

"I can't be sure. Last week he was a little short with some residents at the Research Conference, and this week I've seen him in the halls a couple of times. Tie loose, pants all rumpled as if he slept in them, hair kinda frizzled, but mostly concerned because of his eyes. They were wider than usual and focused a block away. I've seen that look in Bagram on medics and stretcher-bearers. It's like they've just seen too much and want it to stop."

"Do you know what's going on with him?"

"A little. We talked last week; his son graduated high school back in June and is not going to college and has no direction."

"But you told him to join the military, didn't you?"

A pause. Tom smiled grudgingly and said, "Yes, CEO, I did."

"Are you looking for a new 'project'?"

"Whatever are you talking about? I don't have to go looking. Projects are sprouting up all over the place."

"I mean a new 'person project'. Adam has personal difficulties, right? Nothing in the professional realm? And you would like to step into that realm and help him get things settled, right?"

"Of course I would. And I would like to do that before there are professional issues, that's all. 'Project'? Hardly."

"Things have actually been going fairly well recently, haven't they? Sam included?" At the mention of the hospital director's name, Tom again smiled wryly and made some small head nods as he put on his coat.

Sandra went on, "You tell me that the Cardiology Division is running very smoothly and that Mike is doing a good job of running a national search for another cardiologist, right?" Tom nodded, but before he could pick up his briefcase, Sandra said, "And that new disposition ward you created has solved several issues with the training program, and the nursing staff hasn't it?"

Tom smiled more broadly and picked up his briefcase. He knew when he was beaten. And Sandra was so good at it, too. He kissed her goodbye and opened the back door to head for his truck.

Before the door closed, Sandra added, "And that's not even talking about how you got Sam out of that JCAHO problem or . . ."

Tom got in his truck and turned on the motor. Before backing out of the driveway, he stopped to consider what Sandra had raised. Was he looking for some 'project' to keep busy? He didn't think so, but Sandra had been pretty much on target on so many things and for so many times before, and he knew he couldn't just ignore her concerns. He decided it called for a leisurely drive to New City by going through neighborhoods to enjoy fall colors and Halloween decorations, allowing his mind to wander over several thoughts. And one of those thoughts was definitely going to be how to approach Adam Schlecter to find out what was really going on with him.

Tom often took the neighborhood route from the north of town to get to New City. He didn't particularly mind driving on the Interstate since he was well protected and somewhat above the rest of that traffic in his five-year-old F-150. He frequently took the interstate when he was pressed for time, even though his memory seemed to suggest that it was always those times when the traffic was most congested and slowest. Whenever he felt he had the time, however, Tom liked the neighborhood drive. He was a huge fan of porches, expressly ones that span the front width of the house. Even more, he liked those that wrapped around the corner of the house. So, his drive off the interstate was not a set route, he took many turns and even found himself occasionally in dead-end streets. But he didn't care because these trips were not for the express purpose of getting somewhere at a certain time. He drove through the neighborhoods for the ride and the view. He also treasured the time to think.

Tom recalled his distinguished career in the U.S. Air Force Medical Corps and thought of the many times he had solved certain problems emphasizing getting principal players involved in coming up with the solution. His promotions usually mentioned his ability to 'lead'. They also credited him with one or more solutions to thorny problems faced by the command. He recalled that on most of those occasions, Sandra had been there and later would remind him that all he really did was get the people involved to work out the issues and create their own resolution. Probably the only time he didn't get that opinion from her was during his time in Bagram as an operating orthopedic surgeon for war-injured men. And he had really missed her feedback, then.

As he drove, Tom came to the obvious conclusion that Sandra was, once again, correct in her assessment of his concern about Adam Schlecter. Not that Tom was seeking a 'project' but that he probably should cease being too pushy about Adam's state of mind. He should just let Adam know he was concerned and let the man decide if he wanted help. That seemed to be an appropriate and good decision; he reached that decision just as he left residential Cincinnati. He took East McMillan past the University of Cincinnati over to West McMillan and went around Fairview Park to Western Hills Viaduct. From there, he had direct access to the road north to New City Hospital on the site of the old Railroad Hospital.

CHAPTER 3

Monday, October 12

Bonnie Phillips was a very dependable laboratory technician. She had worked in Dr. Schlecter's research lab for seven years, he relied heavily on her to see to the completion of the experiments and all necessary documentation. Bonnie was a little compulsive about these things, which Dr. Schlecter appreciated, especially now that the research had progressed to the point of creating the implantable 'balloons'. Each balloon required careful attention to its ingredients and to the innovative process of forming the actual compartment.

Bonnie was thirty-three years old and already had a reputation for laboratory success before joining Schlecter's operation. She was five foot six inches in height and 160 pounds of determination. Her red hair and green eyes set off her oval face to make an impression of determination and perseverance. Schlecter's success in the project to this point was largely due to the careful attention Bonnie paid each of the key steps.

She was the one that calculated and mixed the proportions of collagen from the tissue bank and the fresh plasma proteins from donors that went into the pre-membrane 'soup. Later, Bonnie was the one to handle the membrane after it coalesced at the bottom of a large mixing tank after heating. She was the one with the careful touch, able to remove the predictable collection of a sheet of proteinaceous material. Bonnie would drain the water from the tank, apply a small amount of dilute acetic acid to the coagulant in the bottom of the tank, and wash the resulting membrane with distilled water.

She had become so careful and talented in handling the resulting product that resembled an ultra-thin and cloudy sheet of Saran Wrap that Schlecter no longer tried to do the next step himself. He had designed a compartment with an upper chamber into which he would place two thin sheets of silicone-coated aluminum that contained several small to medium-sized matched holes. Bonnie would place the newly created membrane on this sheet and smooth it out. When the compartment was closed and air-tight, an operator could create a vacuum in the lower part, and the membrane in the upper chamber would extrude through the holes into the lower chamber. This action created what usually appeared like thin fingers of membrane ballooning into the lower chamber.

At that point, Schlecter would abruptly slide the top aluminum sheet while holding the bottom one stable. This movement caused the ballooning bubbles to close off their opening and float gently to the bottom. After the vacuum was slowly released, Bonnie could gingerly remove the balloons and place them in special containers for filling with various compounds for testing. The testing itself involved placing the bubbles in a container filled with normal saline and sampling the outside fluid every few minutes to determine how much of the compound in the balloon had leaked out.

Bonnie assigned the sampling and testing of compound concentration to the other technician in Schlecter's lab, Terry Demming. Terry was a fairly recent hire of Schlecter's and did not impress Bonnie with having the gentleness of touch to handle the balloons during formation or the filling process, so he was the key person for assembling items in preparation for the challenging steps of membrane preparation and balloon formation and the less difficult steps of sampling and chemical analysis.

Terry was a stocky individual in his early twenties, about five foot ten inches and 180 pounds with a shock of dark hair that always seemed somewhat windblown. He was from Nevada and had come to Ohio to seek admission into one of the state's medical schools. His current goal was to obtain admission into South West Ohio based on a strong recommendation from Dr. Schlecter.

Together, Bonnie and Terry had helped Schlecter produce membranes of varying porosity. They also supported his data collection sufficient to publish several papers on the process and the results. Schlecter had begun to try bubble implantation in rats a few months ago and had determined a series of problems in that model. Most disturbing was the relatively early failure of the bubbles to retain integrity. After three to four days, the membranes had emptied their contents, and the animals were flooded with the antibiotic.

Other problems also developed after bubble implantation: some of the fragile bubbles broke during implantation, the ones that maintained initial integrity were too fragile to be manipulated to give other than a steady-state low concentration of the antibiotic. Shortly after Terry joined the lab, Schlecter decided to try a new technique. He decided to adapt the creation of liposomes containing molecules of interest. The lipid-coat of the liposome changed the dynamics. They had been working with aqueous solutions and concentration gradients. The liposomes changed that to the movement of molecules based on their physical size. Terry's role in recent months had been to develop the process of creating varying size liposomes.

Creating the drug-containing liposomes involved researching the permeability of various liposome membranes and taking the necessary steps to produce them. Terry began this process several months ago. He recently produced repeated batches of liposomes containing antibiotics of interest. His liposomes had a highly reproducible size of 25, 50, or 80 nm. He was excited about this success and looking forward to how Dr. Schlecter would use his work in the balloon technique.

Both technicians were anticipating the usual Monday morning lab meeting where Schlecter would hear of their progress and make plans for the rest of the week. Schlecter arrived three hours later than usual and did not seem interested in their reports. He slouched through the doorway and across the lab to the small area where he had created office space. He neither greeted the technicians nor did he seem to recognize their presence. He slumped in the chair at his desk and put his head in his hands, and sat there almost unmoving.

Terry looked at Bonnie with eyebrows up as if to say, 'What do we do now?"

She shrugged her shoulders and shook her head in reply, and they each returned to the tasks they were doing when he arrived. Over the next hour, their occasional glances into the office confirmed that the only change in Schlecter's position was that he slumped even further on the desk. Neither of them felt it appropriate to interrupt his reverie, and they continued with the work assigned the previous week. At the end of the day, Bonnie approached the office and found Schlecter sleeping with his head on the desk, still wearing the overcoat he had on when he arrived. She decided to leave him alone and signaled to Terry that they should leave without disturbing the boss.

CHAPTER 4

In the hospital bed in New City, the young woman was quite obviously uncomfortable. She turned on her left side with hips and knees flexed, and both hands were clutching at her abdomen.

"Hurts . . ." she moaned.

"The surgical resident at the bedside looked at her and her husband and said, "I know, and we can do something about that very soon. Dr. Schlecter will want to examine your abdomen first. I called him, and he should be here very soon." The resident's voice was calming, but he was thinking, 'I called him almost thirty minutes ago! Where is he?'

The woman's husband asked, "You said she needed surgery, right? Why are we waiting?"

"The surgeon in charge should see her before we go to the operating room. He needs to be aware of her condition and complaints."

"Well, why isn't he here, then?"

"I'm sure that he is on his way."

The husband did not seem as certain of this as did the resident. He leaned toward his wife and took one of her hands.

At that moment, Schlecter entered the room. He was wearing a rumpled suit, and his hair appeared slightly uncombed. His tie was slightly awry, and he had both hands stuffed into the side pockets of the white coat he wore. He walked up to the side of the bed and introduced himself, then turned to the resident and asked, "What do we have?"

Recognizing the need to bring a little more professionalism into the encounter, the resident straightened and began, "A thirty-six-year-old woman, G-2, P-2, both C-sections by Pfannenstiel developed intense abdominal pain 6/10 intensity two days ago shortly after playing volleyball in her yard. Last menstrual period four days prior.

"She presented to the ED in pain with BP 108/65, pulse 110. The abdomen was tense, non-distended, bowel sounds were quiet, no rebound. White count was 8.6, hemoglobin 13.8. Ultrasound was consistent with ovarian cyst with internal hemorrhage."

Schlecter was looking at the woman as this history was presented and he nodded before asking her, "Is the pain any different now?"

"Much worse," she said through gritted teeth.

Schlecter looked at the resident, "And . . .

"And she was admitted for pain control and monitoring. We thought we had the pain under control until this morning when it worsened, and she developed peritoneal signs."

"Ah," Schlecter nodded. He asked the woman, "Can you lie on your back?"

"I'll try." She moved slowly onto her back and gently extended her legs. Schlecter placed his right hand on her abdomen and felt her tense.

"Please try to relax," he said, holding his hand still until he felt her muscles relax. "I'm going to push on you a little here," he said, doing so.

She immediately tensed her muscles, and he quickly removed his hand. As he did, the woman uttered a muffled yelp and moved her hands to prevent him from touching her abdomen again.

"I'm sorry," he said. "I know that hurt. But it tells me that we need to go in there and take care of that problem. I presume you have been told about the need for surgery?" He addressed this question to both the patient and her husband.

As they both indicated agreement, Schlecter turned back to the resident. "Didn't you mention an MRI on the phone?"

"Yes, sir. We thought we could approach this laparoscopically, but I was concerned about the scarring." He indicated that he had originally thought any necessary surgery could be done through a small incision using a laparoscope.

"Why? What scarring?"

"From the Pfannenstiel. It's right in the area where her pain is greatest." The resident referred to the C-section scar that was very low across her abdomen right at the upper level of pubic hair.

"Oh, yeah. Right. Good idea. What did it show?"

"There is a moderate amount of adhesions in the area. We think an open laparotomy would be best."

"We?"

"Uh, the radiologist and me."

"Oh. Well, I need to look at it myself. but I'll probably agree." Schlecter turned back to the husband and wife. "I'm going to look at the MRI, and I'll meet you in the Operating Room. I think the resident here is right, so I would like you to sign consent for an open surgical procedure."

The woman nodded bleakly at him and said, "OK. I had that 'bikini cut' before when I was a lot younger and didn't want a big scar."

"I understand," Schlecter said. "But that scar is now right where we would like to go with a 'scope. I'm afraid that's not going to work with the scars on the inside. I hope you understand."

"Whatever you say, doctor," said the husband.

Schlecter nodded to them and indicated the resident should come with him. They stopped at the nursing station to order the patient transfer to the operating room and then went down the stairs to the Imaging department to view the MRI.

After a brief look at the MRI, Schlecter agreed that an open procedure would be safest. Nursing and anesthesia took care of all the requisite consenting, pre-op abdominal scrubbing, surgical handwashing, and appropriate gowning of all involved.

After a midline incision and use of a retractor to move some of the abdominal contents out of the way, the culprit causing the pain was evident: a seven-centimeter ovarian cyst on the left ovary was filled with blood; some had broken through the cyst wall and leaked into the abdomen.

Schlecter spoke to the resident assisting, "Did you ask her about wanting more kids?"

He nodded, "She's not inclined. That may be the pain but her husband seemed to agree."

"So did she consent to lose this ovary?"

"Yes. She also consented to appendectomy if we want to push for that."

"Let's just do the thing we came to do before taking on something else, OK, doctor?" Schlecter said somewhat dismissively.

The resident nodded and bent to help find the necessary blood vessels to clamp. A couple of times in the next few minutes, the resident noted that Schlecter's hands became still. He looked up to see the surgeon staring into the wound in an unfocused manner. He tapped on Schlecter's instrument with his own, and the surgeon seemed to awaken from faraway thoughts to continue with the ovary removal.

Twice during the removal, Schlecter grabbed the retractor that the resident was using to hold the bowel out of the operative field. He pushed the retractor firmly away from where he was operating to get a better view. Each time he did so, the resident immediately let some of the pressure off because he was worried about harming the underlying bowel. When Schlecter finally made the last deep tie-off of blood vessels and snipped the remaining tissue holding the ovary in place, he lifted it out of the incision so everyone could see.

"Big bugger, lot of bleeding. No wonder it hurt."

They rinsed out the abdomen and were about to close when the resident noted a blood collection where there had not been any moments before. Schlecter blotted it out with some sponges and used the sponges to compress the bowel away from the area. Everyone watched for a full minute and saw no further bleeding, so Schlecter allowed the bowel to return to normal and asked for a sponge count. When the was finished and complete, he turned to the resident and said, "You can close. I'll go see the husband."

CHAPTER 5

Thursday, October 22

Two hours later, the young woman was tucked into bed in the recovery area and was sound asleep. She had started to awaken from the anesthesia but had complained of intense pain and was given an ordered dose of morphine. She slept.

The nurse checking her vital signs routinely a short time later noted that her blood pressure was lower than on admission to the unit and the pulse slightly higher. She decided to recheck those measurements sooner than required. Sure enough, five minutes later, the blood pressure was 86/44, the pulse was 110. The patient was not rousable. The nurse immediately called the resident, and they both hovered over the patient's bed.

After checking the wound for evidence of bleeding and finding none, and checking the blood pressure himself, the resident went to the nurses' station and tried to call Schlecter. There was no answer either to his cell phone or to the number given as his home phone. The resident called back on the cell phone, left a detailed message about the patient's condition, and then went back into the patient's room.

The nurse looked up and said, "Her BP is now 76 over palpable and real thready pulse."

"They pulled the sheet back and again checked the wound that remained clear. The resident thought the abdomen looked more distended than when he closed the wound and pulled the patient's top up to examine her abdomen more fully. That's when he appreciated the bruising look on her flanks and around the top of the wound bandage.

The nurse looked at the bruising and asked, "What's that from?"

The resident brusquely replied, "That's called Cullen's sign. It means she's bleeding into her abdomen. We've gotta get her back in the OR!"

The nurse scurried to get help to move the patient. She told someone to alert the Operating Room.

The resident called Schlecter's cell phone again. Still no answer. He left another terse message and then he ran up the stairs to scrub for surgery.

Opening the wound was not difficult; it only involved snipping his previous sutures. The wound promptly fell open. Blood gushed out of the abdomen startling everyone in the room.

"Get me some suction and get her typed for four units STAT," the resident called. He focused solely on finding the source of bleeding for the next fifteen minutes. The bleeding initially appeared brisk. The abdomen was suctioned to remove the blood but was never successful in creating a clean field of view to allow the resident to find the offending bleeder. He packed the wound with large dressings and tried to move the bowel out of the way to visualize underneath but could not see adequately. The anesthesiologist noted the ever-falling blood pressure with mounting concern in his voice. The ordered units of blood were pumped in with little discernible change in the pressure until the last unit was completed. Then the flow of blood began to perceptibly slow. For a brief moment, the resident thought he had a chance to close the leak. Even as he pushed the bowel out of the way and applied new large dressings to the area, the anesthesiologist said, "Her pulse just went to zero. She's flatlining."

"Push fluids," called the resident. But the others in the room recognized the futility at that point and slowly moved their hands off the body.

The anesthesiologist spoke directly to the surgical resident, "Danny. It's over, man. We lost."

The resident looked at the monitors. The meaning of the zero readings for blood pressure and pulse was clear. The flat line of the electrocardiogram underscored the truth. His heart sunk. They really had lost. His patient was dead. And he didn't know why.

The scrub nurse reached over and took the retractor out of his hand, and started collecting the instruments while the circulating nurse stepped up and started pulling the dressings and packing out of the wound. No one called for a sponge count.

The resident stepped back from the body and started to pull off his gloves. The circulating nurse asked, "Are you going to talk to the family?"

He nodded and left the operating room, shoulders slumped.

Chapter 6

Friday, October 23

Friday, October 23

Normally, Tom Bolling enjoyed his drive to work at New City. Sitting in his F-150 put him in his favorite perch, above the rest of the commuting public, giving him an enhanced vision of the traffic between him and his objective. Tom considered himself a man of vision, and being able to see what the traffic was doing a mile ahead allowed him an opportunity to make alternative decisions; he liked that feeling of being in charge. But that was not what he felt now, certainly not in charge of the situation that blew out of control the previous evening.

He had been called by the Administrative Officer of the Day shortly after supper and notified of an operative death involving one of the surgical residents. It took a second call to the Operating Room for him to hear the full story and realize Adam Schlecter's involvement and absence. Tom had called Adam at home and got no answer and then did a quick telephone interview with the surgical resident and the scrub nurse who assisted in the second operation.

As he drove toward the hospital that morning, Tom was already formulating courses of action in his mind. First, there was the issue of a Sentinel Event notification to make to the Joint Commission for Accreditation of Healthcare Organizations. Such a report was not mandatory but definitely in the best interests of a hospital to do so. New City's accreditation status with the JCAHO was important; without full accreditation, they could not collect Medicare funding, and the academic affiliation with South West Ohio Medical School might be canceled. Once New City lost Medicare funding approval, all commercial insurance would follow. He knew that the single Sentinel Event would not lose New City its accreditation. However, he also knew that the hospital had been on a six-month survey report status pending complete accreditation just a year ago. That decision led him to establish an in-house immediate After Action Review for any cardiac arrest. Subsequently, New City received full accreditation. Nonetheless, Tom knew the JCHO might look harder at their Sentinel Event because of that experience.

Tom knew The JCAHO would expect a full Root Cause analysis when he filed the Sentinel Event. He intended to invoke his After Action Review concept to provide the necessary analysis, and he began to remind himself of all the players he would have to assemble. That made him wonder again about Adam Schlecter. He had been present for the initial surgery but then seemed to have vanished. Tom intended to run that concern to ground himself.

He would have to have 'all the ducks in a row' before filing that report with the JCAHO.

He pulled into the parking deck at New City with many of the issues resolved in his mind, many but not all. Fortunately, he had called Beverly earlier that morning to get her started on some of the administrative actions necessary. As he strode through the lobby thinking about the problems of the day, he almost missed the high sign from Nick, his favorite barista at the Green Bean kiosk.

"Usual, Big Doc?"

"Sure, Nick. Thanks for catching me," Tom said, sliding over to the cash register to pay. When Nick finished preparing Tom's usual, he brought it over to the register and said, "You look troubled. Should I have put some Irish whiskey in that?"

"Not for the start of the day, Nick. But I sure may need it at the end." Tom saluted Nick with the cup and continued to his office.

His long-time secretary, Mary Brighthouse, looked up when he entered and said, "Bev has already tipped me off. I'm setting up the AAR with folks right after the morning meeting."

"Good plan," Tom said, shucking off his overcoat and entering his office. "Can you buzz Beverly for me?"

Mary did so, and before Tom could hang up his coat and get to his desk, Beverly Hancock walked in. Beverly, at five foot two with gray streaks in her hair, might be mistaken for a librarian seeking an overdue book. She was, however, the strong right arm of Tom Bolling, Chief of Staff. Beverly had experience working in several departments in New City over the years, mostly clinical ones. She had invaluable insight into the processes behind the support services. She also knew the thinking that drove most of the administrative services. She felt aligned with Tom on the 'clinical side', but she considered herself an administrator, and a very good one. Tom agreed with her assessment and considered her his best chance of succeeding in his job.

"Where are we?" he asked without preamble.

"First, there's nothing else important coming up at the morning meeting. Second, it seems that everyone has heard about the death and probably has their own version of the events."

"I don't doubt that. I'm sure that Roslyn has all the necessary facts to prove that the nursing staff cannot be blamed," Tom said, referring to the Chief Nurse, Roslyn Burke. "What have you got on the JCAHO?"

"I printed the Sentinel Event Policy out," she said, handing him a folder, "and the pertinent fact is you have 45 days to tell them about it if you decide to do so. I highlighted that part."

"I expect a lot of that will depend on Sam's attitude and whatever we get from the AAR." Tom took a deep draught on his coffee. "Boy, that's good," he said, grinning. "Maybe the only thing I'm going to like about this whole day."

"Don't give up on it just yet," Beverly said, preceding him to the conference room for the morning meeting.

Chapter 7

Friday, October 23

Sam Mastone held a morning meeting at New City each weekday at 0800. Players at the meeting were the Chief Nurse and her Assistant Chief, Alena Preston, Tom and his executive assistant, Beverly, and recently, Sam's executive assistant, Holly Ellington, a recent graduate of a Master's in Healthcare Administration. Sam had added Holly to his team to be the interface between him and directors of various administrative departments. Most department heads were less than enthusiastic about explaining their business and their reasoning to a recent graduate. One, in particular, the Chief Financial Officer, Karl Breslinger, actually refused to talk to Holly on business matters.

The routine was always the same; all the players assembled in the conference room by 0758 and took their accustomed seats. Tom and Beverly on the right-hand side of the table, and the nurses sat on the left directly across from them. Tom didn't particularly like the seating that created an 'opposition' atmosphere, but he wasn't certain how to change it. Holly usually came in with Sam and sat to his immediate left at the head of the table to take notes.

At exactly 0800 the door into the director's office would open and Sam would enter carrying the several page report on the activities in the hospital over the previous twenty-four hours, the "G. and L.

Report." This report, of Gains and Losses, reported in a tabular format all the admissions to the hospital and all the discharges plus visits to various clinics and the Emergency Department. Gains and Losses were reported by individual wards but aggregated for the hospital. The statistics included the number of vacant beds on each ward as of midnight.

This report was produced by the Administrative Officer of the Day shortly after midnight from automated data, printed, and circulated so that it was readily available to everyone from the Director to the clerk in the ED no later than 0700.

Yet, every morning Sam Mastone would enter the conference room at 0800 with this report in his hand carefully studying it as if it had just appeared. He nodded to everyone, sat at the head of the table, and said, "Well, with the one exception, things seem to be going alright." The one exception to which he referred was, of course, the operative death. Sam looked first at Roslyn and then at Tom and asked, "can you tell me what happened?"

Taking his clue from Sam's line of sight, Tom spoke first. "Not completely. The basics are a young woman bled into an ovarian cyst, and it leaked into the abdomen, so an oophorectomy was done around mid-day yesterday . . ."

"Hold it," Sam interjected. "What's that about an 'OOfer'?"

"That's the surgical term for removal of an ovary," Tom said, again surprised at the lack of clinical terminology knowledge by the director of the hospital. He continued, "So an oophorectomy was done yesterday. The patient was returned to the operating room in the early evening when she developed intra-abdominal bleeding. The operating resident could not find the bleeder. She expired in the operating room."

"Resident? There was only a resident doing that operation?" Sam was raising the important question.

"At the time, the situation was seen as emergent, and he took control."

"Except that his control didn't have a good outcome, right? Where was the attending?"

As Sam asked this, Tom recognized that the director knew full well that Adam Schlecter had not shown up for the patient's return to the operating room. Sam's previous question had not been totally innocent. Tom thought he could see a corner of Roslyn's mouth tip upward, but she refrained from an actual smile; Tom realized he was about to be blind-sided. Tom slowly shook his head and said, "I don't have that information right now. I have an AAR scheduled with the key personnel right after this meeting and should have more information very soon."

Roslyn sniffed, "That's why you are holding my nurses here long after their shift has ended?"

"Their input into the AAR is critical. You know that Roslyn," Tom said soothingly.

Roslyn was having none of it, however. "If it was so important, why couldn't you have done your little review right after the death occurred? That's what you do during the day shift, isn't it?" Roslyn was stating an obvious truth but implying something else. She was not a fan of Tom's AAR protocol, claiming that it took time away from nursing duties. She was pushing Tom to admit that he didn't want to come to the hospital in the middle of the night to perform the AAR, and that was why the nurses had to stay past the end of their shift.

Not addressing her implicit question directly, Tom said, "I thought it best to have this review involve not only those in the operating room but also Dr. Song and the attending. I believe we have a better chance to find those important people this morning rather than last night."

Roslyn seemed surprised by the mention of the pathologist, Monique Song, being included in the AAR and became quiet. Tom took that opportunity to say, "And, if there is no other pressing business, perhaps I should go get that underway right now?" He leaned forward as if to rise from his chair as he looked at Sam.

The director looked back and forth between Tom and Roslyn and then nodded. Tom quickly got to his feet, and he and Beverly left the conference room.

CHAPTER 8

They assembled in a small conference room near the operating suite. Tom asked the Day Supervisor to join the discussion. None of the surgical nurses had ever participated in one of the AAR activities in the past since they were only done following a cardiac arrest and involved the members of the arrest response team. Since the inception of the program, all such events had occurred only on the wards and usually only on the Medicine Service. After brief introductions, Tom gave a short history of the AAR and explained how he intended it to be implemented.

Two years previously, a JCAHO review of New City had identified shortcomings in the hospital's review of cardiac arrests and codes and cited the facility for this. Tom, as a relatively new chief of staff at the time, created a new program to have a senior staff physician attend every code during regular hours to observe and to oversee a detailed review of all actions after the code ended. The 'after-action review', or AAR, was patterned after the similar military procedure because Tom was never going to be anything other than a military physician, which he had been for 22 years, and a general officer, which he had been for four.

Initially, the program irritated the senior physicians. The teaching aspects slowly made an impression on almost everyone. The nursing leaders were not supportive. They felt the nursing time involved was not useful for the nurses. Tom presented the background to get the operating room nurses interested in the teaching aspects of the program.

He explained the event in question was to be told by actual observers in chronologic order, with all parties contributing. In all previous AARs, the team had two additional items. One was the printout from the cardiac monitor. The other was a medication list kept by a nurse during the resuscitation. Neither such record was available for this case, so Tom expressed the need for everyone to do their best to remember events, including the use of instruments, medications administered, and orders given.

Everyone took the process seriously. Tom asked that the storyline begin with the events in the recovery room and the surgical resident being called to the bedside. The recovery nurse recounted the falling blood pressure and rising pulse and how she and the resident had checked the wound for bleeding and noted the swollen abdomen with bruising. The resident confirmed Cullen's sign and said his examination showed a distended, tense abdomen with absent bowel sounds. He thought a fluid wave was present, indicating a large amount of fluid in the cavity.

Various individuals recounted how notification occurred to the operating room, and how they mobilized for an emergency laparotomy. Additional parts of the story involved the patient's transfer to the operating room, transfer to the table, and preparation of the abdomen, while the resident and scrub nurse were getting gowned and gloved. Tom stopped the discussion once to confirm with everyone who handled the patient that she had remained stuporous. The anesthesiologist confirmed a lack of response before she put the patient to sleep.

Again, all hands agreed on the large volume of blood that came from the newly opened wound. The story got somewhat tangled after that as the resident tried to tell his maneuvers to find the bleeding point and the circulating nurse told of the suction in the wound. Everyone agreed on the large number of dressings and sponges used to clean the operative field, and every speaker agreed that all possible efforts were made to find the point of bleeding without success. The anesthesiologist had the only written record of events and noted when the blood was transfused and what minimal response was obtained. Her record showed the exact time of the loss of vital signs.

Beverly had been both recording the conversation but also taking some notes. She looked at Tom when the conversation ceased. He looked like he had lost two days of sleep; his eyes were red, and his hair was ruffled from him running his hand through it so often. Still, he looked each person in the eye and asked, "What else could have been done?"

There were no plausible suggestions. Everyone present agreed that they in the aggregate and the resident, in particular, did everything possible to identify the source of blood loss. They had simply failed to do so soon enough to prevent the death of the young woman.

Tom thanked them all for their participation in the attempt to save this young woman's life and for their helpfulness in determining what had actually happened in the operating room the night before. Each person thanked him for the opportunity to be useful in providing a close examination of her death; they filed from the room, leaving only Beverly and the resident with Tom.

"Are you all right?" Beverly asked.

"I will be," Tom replied. "I'm just having some flashbacks to young men dying on my operating table in Bagram. It's tough on everybody."

After a short silence, the resident spoke. "Sir," he said. "If I may be so bold, I really don't think the problem was what we just discussed here. We need to have this same discussion with everyone involved in the initial operation. I really believe we may have left the bleeder active when we closed after the oophorectomy."

Tom looked at the young man steadily for a moment. "You are right, of course. We have only looked at the sharp end of the spear. I suspect you're correct about the error occurring earlier. I intend to do exactly what you suggest when I ever find Dr. Schlecter."

"Yes, sir." The resident nodded and left the conference room.

Beverly looked at Tom for a brief moment and wondered aloud if he needed another Black Eye. He smiled wryly at her and asked her to meet him in his office with Monique Song in thirty minutes. He intended to go for a short walk.

CHAPTER 9

Friday, October 23

Tom didn't pay a lot of attention to his steps as he walked around the hospital for the next quarter-hour. He entered the lobby where Nick and the coffee kiosk would have certainly attracted him, if he allowed that. But he wanted to be alone with his thoughts and to try to untangle the mystery of Adam Schlecter's absence. In the lobby, Tom turned away from the Green Bean and walked toward the maze of tunnels that led to all the other areas of the hospital. He walked quickly through the Emergency Department, nodding briskly to individuals who caught his eye, signaling he was not there to chat. He even went to the loading dock and watched the unloading of a truck of pharmaceuticals. Then, Tom went on a walk through the first floor hallways. As he came around a hallway corner, he realized he was near the Research Wing and decided to go to Adam's laboratory to talk with his technicians about his absence.

He entered the lab and was immediately struck by the activity involving the two technicians. They were each scurrying around, moving containers of specimens and collecting their notebooks. Tom addressed Bonnie from across the cabinet where she was compiling her written notes.

"Bonnie? Can I talk to you for a minute?"

"What? Oh, hi, Dr. Bolling. I didn't see you come in. What's up?"

"I said, could I talk to you for a moment?"

"Right now, we're about to have a weekly meeting and get new assignments. Can it wait?"

"Probably so. I'm just concerned about Adam."

"Yeah," she nodded vigorously, "we were, too."

Tom picked up on the change in verb tense. "You were? Worried about him, I mean."

"Oh yeah, sure. All the moping around and missing weekly meetings." Her use of the past tense caught Tom's interest.

"What happened to change your mind?" he asked.

"Well, he came in today like the old guy. Chipper and upbeat and ready for giving us new work to do."

"What?" Tom was incredulous. "Adam came in today?"

"Yeah, sure. He's right back there in his office." Bonnie pointed to the back corner of the lab. The top of Adam's head was visible over some boxes piled up next to his desk.

Tom blinked a couple of times and said to Bonnie and Terry, "Your meeting with Dr. Schlecter will be postponed for a while. Better find something else to occupy your time." Then he strode over to the office area and called out from the doorway, "Adam, where in tarnation have you been?"

Schlecter looked up and smiled at Tom. "Hey, Tom. What brings you down to the lab?"

Tom was almost dumbfounded. "Adam, are you not aware that we have been looking for you since last night?"

"Looking for me? What for?" The puzzled expression on Adam's face was not an act. Tom paused for a second and then continued with slightly less force to his voice.

"Your surgical patient crashed last night and had to go back to the O.R. The resident called your cell and your home. No answer. I tried your home phone early this morning and got no answer. Where were you?"

"Uh, I'm sorry. I didn't know anybody was looking for me."

"Answer me. Where the hell were you?"

"Uh, I actually was at home."

"Not answering the telephone? What's going on, Adam?"

"Ah, I gotta tell you, Tom, things have gotten worse. My son ran away from home last weekend. My wife and I are depressed. I turned all the phones off, and we took some sleeping pills."

"What? How responsible was that? You had a patient in the recovery room."

"I know. I know. She was stable in the O.R. I told her husband she'd sleep things off and be just fine. What happened? Why did she go back to the O.R.?"

"She bled in her belly, Adam. Probably her whole blood volume from the story I got. Your resident took her back and released a tidal wave of blood by opening the wound. He gave her four units and never found the bleeder." Tom's biting presentation and fixed stare were telling on Adam, who seemed to get smaller. "She died, Adam. In the O.R. I just completed an AAR on the second operation."

Adam slumped against his desk. "She died?"

"Yes. Early this morning and you were nowhere to be found. I want a real explanation, Adam."

"Yeah, yeah. Of course. Sure. I mean, I told you. We just turned everything off and slept. Who talked to her husband?"

"Your resident took care of all that."

"Oh God, what'm I gonna do?"

"Well, the first thing you're going to do is get yourself over to my office. Monique is meeting me there. We will rehash the oophorectomy with you, the resident, the scrub nurse, the circulator, and the anesthesiologist. I'm doing a second AAR on this case. And you're the primary witness."

CHAPTER 10

They gathered in Tom's office, Adam Schlecter, the resident, the scrub nurse, the circulating nurse, and the anesthesiologist from the original procedure, Beverly and Dr. Monique Song.

Dr. Song, chief of Laboratory Service at New City, was also the head of the Anatomic Pathology Section. Monique was only five foot four inches but somehow always seemed taller and a larger personality than that. Her Philipino heritage was evident in her face, and her usual style was to have her hair swept back in a bun. Tom had not been responsible for recruiting her to New City; she had arrived at least four years before he took the job as chief of staff. She had come from Cleveland, where she had functioned as the medical examiner for Cuyahoga County for five years. Her reputation of being thoroughly organized and thorough made her a reliable witness in those cases where testimony was needed. When she moved into the private sector at New City, furthermore, she brought old habits with her. She maintained a system of specimen collection and systematic documentation of 'chain of custody' on all tissue and blood samples as if she expected to be called back into court.

Dr. Song had not made many friends in the hospital until Tom Bolling arrived. He persuaded her to reduce her focus from keeping others out of her domain to preserve a legal chain of custody. Tom wanted her to provide students, residents, and staff physicians the answers they were seeking. In a short time, she had actually become good at teaching, albeit somewhat lengthy in her discussions. She was very proud of the teaching award she received two years ago and of her new reputation. Nonetheless, residents knew better than to drop into the lab for a brief chat.

Monique did not usually attend AARs. Tom had asked for her to be present this time because he wanted her to do an autopsy immediately afterward. She normally would become acquainted with the care that preceded death on those patients she autopsied by review of the medical record and radiographs. Tom thought she would need information that might not be present in the record to help determine the cause of death in this instance.

The resident provided the initial history and physical findings on the patient. He recapped the short hospitalization with increasing pain to the point where Dr. Schlecter came to see the patient. The MRI results were presented, and he defended his decision to operate. Schlecter said his pre-operative intent was a simple cystectomy. He explained how the operative findings changed his mind about the goal. He and the resident commented about the reasons to proceed to an oophorectomy. The scrub nurse and the resident mentioned the bleeding deep in the wound. Various players told their version of how the surgeons addressed the free blood in the wound.

Monique asked twice about the retractor placement on the bowel and the timing of the retraction during the period before closing the wound. The resident mentioned the two times he had been asked to provide more traction on the bowel than he was comfortable applying. The scrub nurse noted that the observation time to determine if the bleeding was a problem was 'only' about a minute. The resident added that during that time he was again providing traction.

By the time the AAR was finished, Adam Schlecter was sweating profusely, and his face was flushed. His voice tended to rise in the conversation, and he was visibly trembling at times. Tom asked each person in the review to answer the question, 'Was everything done properly?' The scrub nurse and the resident felt that they should have paid more attention to assure that the bleeding was not active before closing. The circulating nurse and the anesthesiologist were non-committal, and Adam thought everything was done 'by the book'. That comment made Tom raise his eyebrows, and Monique made a minimal shake of her head.

Tom thanked everyone for their help and active participation and excused the nurses, the resident, and the anesthesiologist. He waited until they had closed the door behind them and turned to Monique. "Are you prepared to do the post?"

"Give me twenty minutes to change, and I will be," she said, standing and moving toward the doorway.

"Thanks," Tom said, smiling at her. "We'll be right down."

She left the room. Schlecter started to stand, but Tom stopped him. "I expect you to accompany me to the autopsy, Adam."

"What for? We know she's gonna find some bleeder in there. Nothing I could have done."

"Is that really going to be your story? Are you going to stand there and say, 'Not my fault' when you were the surgeon of record? Are you certain there is nothing for you to learn from this, Adam?"

"Well . . . I mean. Uh, maybe."

"Maybe what, Adam? Maybe you'll go with me? Maybe you made a mistake? Maybe what?"

"Maybe I'll go with you. Can't hurt."

"Good choice." Turning to Beverly, Tom asked, "Would you mind coming, too?"

"If you wish," she said.

Less than a half-hour later, the four of them were standing at the table where the abdominal wound was laid open. Monique had collected a Deaver retractor from the operating room and had it at the table. With the abdomen open as it would have been for the oophorectomy, Monique asked Schlecter, "Where was the retractor placed?"

"Well, I'm not sure. I was looking in the field."

"You said, and the resident agreed, you needed more retraction to see."

"Well, yes, I guess."

"So, where did you need to see, and where was the retractor?"

Schlecter took a deep breath and stepped closer to the table. He picked up the retractor, placed it against the bowel, and pulled it up toward the patient's right shoulder. "About like that, I think. You could've asked the resident where it was."

"I wanted to know where you thought it was, Adam," Monique said. She then used the retractor to maneuver the bowel out of the way and expose the mesentery. "I doubt if you can appreciate the torn mesenteric vein at this time," she said, pointing to the profuse field of blood vessels connected to the bowel. "But even before I heard the AAR, I thought the story sounded like a mesenteric vessel torn from retraction. So I did a little investigation of my own."

Monique turned to face Tom. "You're probably going to hear about this soon. I took this young woman's body to the Imaging department and did a quick post-mortem abdominal angiogram. Charlie wasn't the happiest, but I convinced him it was necessary. If you would turn on those view boxes behind you, I'll show you what happened here."

Tom did as she asked, and Monique stepped up to the box with a pointer that magically appeared in her hand. She traced the flow of blood saying, "Here you see the abdominal aorta and the superior and inferior mesenteric arteries. Notice the flush of the contrast material into the small arterial loops and then . . ." she put the end of the pointer on a patch of white that did not look like a blood vessel. "Here you see the leak from mesenteric veins into the peritoneum."

Adam said quickly, "That could have happened anytime." He was clearly in defensive mode.

Tom rejoined just as quickly, "You know that's not true, Adam. You had a bleeder. That vein was likely torn by aggressive retraction. When it bled you compressed it with the retraction and closed the wound without insuring your patient's safety."

Adam flushed again and said, "That's not fair, I . . ."

"Cut it out, Adam. Now. You and I will deal with this, and I want you and Newberry in my office in thirty minutes. This is a serious Sentinel Event, and the JCAHO is going to be all over us for this."

CHAPTER 11

Friday, October 23

A short time later, they were all back in Tom's office. Sam Newberry was in the overstuffed 'dignitary' chair, and Adam was in a straight-backed chair in front of Tom's desk. Tom was behind his desk, and Beverly was in a chair from her office brought in for the occasion. No one was smiling.

Tom started the conversation, speaking directly to Adam, "You have created a very serious problem for us, are you aware of that?"

Adam nodded jerkily and started to speak, but Tom held up his hand. "I don't want to hear any more of the 'it's not my fault' routine. This is every bit your fault; that's what being the surgeon of record is all about."

Adam looked down at the floor and made no effort to rebut.

"Just so you are aware," Tom went on, "the problem you created is an operative death. An operative death is considered a Sentinel Event by the Joint Commission. Consequently, this hospital, meaning me, will have to file a report with them very soon. Do you know what is entailed in such a report, Adam?"

His bent head muffled Adam's response of "No."

Tom went on, "It involves me providing them with a full and thorough report of what happened including what they call a 'Root Cause Analysis' to determine what caused the death. A Root Cause Analysis is a tedious process and involves several individuals and puts the entire event and all players out in the common conversation. There will be no mistake about who caused the problem."

Adam sat almost immovable.

Tom went on, "I have now heard from two different groups involved in this patient's care. The operative group in the OR at the time of her death and the one gathered for the initial surgery. And, finally, I have been able to add the input from the surgeon of record."

"I understand that you had some trouble seeing down into the operative field, but it is clear to me that you insisted on too much pull on the retractor." Tom turned to Newberry and said, "Monique was able to demonstrate a tear in a mesenteric vein, and even though Adam and the resident were aware of bleeding into the field at the end of the oophorectomy, he closed without ensuring that bleeding had stopped."

Adam could not retrain himself. "It had stopped," he insisted. "There was no bleeding before we started to close."

"I contend you don't know that," Tom said. "You put pressure on the area while observing, right?"

"Well . . ."

"Right?"

"Uh, yeah, the resident was . . ."

"Again, no excuses. You were the surgeon of record. You knew there had been slow bleeding in the field, and you allowed your observation to occur with pressure on the bowel. Didn't you?"

After a clenched jaw moment, Adam gritted out, "Yes."

"And during the surgery, the resident said you stopped and stared, and he had to tap your instrument to get your attention. What was that all about?"

Adam shifted in his chair and looked quickly at Newberry and then back at the floor. "I was, uh. Just thinking about what we were doing."

Sam Newberry sat forward in his chair and asked, "Adam, was this what we talked about?"

Tom looked at Sam with his eyebrows closing together, "You know something about this, Sam?"

"Adam, are you going to speak up?" the chairman of surgery asked.

Adam just sat with eyes downcast again.

Tom said, "Sam, what is this all about?"

Sam then mentioned to Tom that a couple of the residents had come to him in the past couple of months and mentioned that Adam had stopped in the middle of an operation and stared into the distance for a minute or more.

"How many times had this happened?" Tom wanted to know.

"Well, each of them reported two cases to me. They had talked to each other and realized the occurrences were not limited to their experience and decided to tell me."

"And . . .?"

"And, I called Adam in and discussed the events with him. He told me he was very tired and had just needed to stop and think about what was going on."

"And you believed him?"

"Well, yes, I did. But I told him that such things could not continue. I also told him he would be watched."

"Uh-huh." Tom sat back in his chair and fixed Newberry with an unblinking stare. "And who was doing the watching, Sam?"

"Well, I arranged for him to operate only with one of our senior residents and they were to tell me whether there was a problem."

"That was not one of the senior residents on the case last night, was it?"

Newberry cleared his throat and said, "Uh, no. One of the junior ones asked for a consult and got Adam, and I didn't know about it."

"So, now I find out that one of our surgeons is having staring spells in the operating room and the chief of surgery knows all about that and was waiting for … what? For things to get worse? Well, they just did." Sam sat up straight in his chair and asked self-importantly, "Well, what do you expect me to do, Tom?"

Tom's answer was cold and to the point. "I expect you to do your job. I expect you to protect patient safety, and I expect you to manage the privileges in your service in a manner that meets professional standards."

Sam Newberry sat back in the chair as if Tom had slapped him..

Tom continued, "Adam may not know about the findings of the JCAHO visit two years ago, but you certainly did. The head of that team was upset with our reviews of in-house codes, you remember. His father had died from an in-house code, and he was not happy with our handling of codes. He almost held up our accreditation until I told him we would start the AAR process for every code. And we appear to have weathered that issue.

"Do either of you know what would happen to this hospital if we lost our JCAHO accreditation?"

Both surgeons shrugged and shook their heads.

"Well, one thing you wouldn't like about it is we would lose the ability to continue our affiliation with the medical school and its training program!"

The surgeons were clearly unaware of that consequence and somewhat troubled that Tom might be preparing to tell them that the affiliation was to be terminated. Instead, he said, "Residency and other training programs cannot give credit for time spent in an unaccredited facility. Your surgical residents would disappear the next day."

He went on, "And we would no longer be able to collect government funds for care, like Medicare and Medicaid. And all the private insurers would follow suit. Sam Mastone would command me to fire whoever was responsible for that cascade of events. And then, he would expect me to fire myself."

A significant chill fell on the room, and neither Sam nor Adam wanted to face Tom as he continued. "Sam, I expect you will have this man's surgical privileges severely revoked until he can demonstrate the character and ability to resume them. Plus, I want a full accounting, in writing, from you no later than Monday afternoon detailing exactly what went on with those resident reports and how you will react differently in the future when something like that occurs. That written report should also itemize the department's actions against Dr. Schlecter and how he will be observed and monitored in the future."

Adam looked up at Tom and then at his chairman. "You can't do this to me. It's like putting a knife to my throat."

Tom responded immediately. "Adam, this was all your fault. I'm not going to say something about 'you should have thought of that' because it appears to me that you weren't thinking much at all. You caused a death and a huge problem for Sam, for me, and the hospital. I'm going to spend a lot of time I don't really have with the Joint Commission to keep us open and accredited. I don't have time for your whining and griping because you got caught."

Adam leaped to his feet. "It's all a bunch of crap, and you both know it. I'm getting punished here, and it's really not my fault. You are cutting my throat and acting all sanctimonious about it. I'm done with this." He followed these words with a quick exit slamming the door behind him.

Tom didn't change his expression as he looked at the chairman of surgery. "Go do your job," he said and did not rise as Newberry left the room.

CHAPTER 12

Wednesday, November 11

Sam Mastone made his usual punctual arrival at the morning meeting, looked briefly at the daily report, and said, "Looks like it was a quiet night," and took his seat at the head of the table. Holly Ellington trailed him into the room and took her usual seat to Sam's left. Sam looked expectantly at Tom and Roslyn, and she spoke first.

"I believe we are seeing some of our first cases of influenza."

Tom's eyebrows rose.

The Chief Nurse went on, "Several of my nurses are out today with fever and chills. There have been two cases of similar symptoms in the hospital recently."

Tom asked, "Do you know if they had their flu shots?"

"I do not."

"It's a bit early for the flu season but not impossible."

"Are you suggesting these nurses are faking?" Roslyn huffed up and stared at Tom.

Tom just shook his head gently and said, "Of course not, Roslyn. I'm saying we really need to get a handle on this if it really is the seasonal flu. I hadn't heard anything about admissions who had proved flu, but I'm pretty sure that the campaign for getting all the staff to get their flu shots is just getting started. We may have a serious shortage of nurses and physicians and technicians if we don't get everyone covered right away."

"Well, I will announce to everyone in Nursing that they need to get their flu shot. Can the Employee Health cover that?"

"I don't know," Tom said and then looked at Beverly, who nodded that she understood the question and the need for an answer. She got up and left the room as she pulled out her cell phone.

Tom turned to Sam. "You may recall we had a similar problem two years ago when the vaccine turned out to be only about 10% effective."

"You told me that was because the virus had mutated or something," Sam countered.

"Which was true, and that is why the vaccine was not effective. But whether it's a mutation or lack of vaccination, we could definitely have a problem here." Turning back to Roslyn he asked, "Could you find out if those nurses had a flu shot?"

"Yes, of course."

Beverly came back into the room and noted, "James in Employee Health said they have only a few doses. He also told me that local drug stores, grocery stores, and pharmacies are well-stocked and can handle walk-ins. Our employee health insurance covers the shot."

Tom turned back to Sam. "Let's get an all employee bulletin out reminding everyone of the immediate need to get their flu shots."

Sam nodded and looked at Holly, who was busily writing things in her notebook.

Sam said, "Anything else? Something good, perhaps?"

Tom spoke. "I had a good conversation with the Joint Commission yesterday. The Executive Vice President for Accreditation is a retired Army Colonel and a friend of mine. He said the feeling in the Board Room about our Sentinel Event is that we have done the right thing and are considered appropriately covered."

"Why do you know some Army colonel?"

"We took a few courses together at the War College. He's also in the medical corps, and he's a good man."

Sam nodded and went on, "So they are not planning on coming back and doing another site visit?"

"Not according to Ernie. He said they were properly impressed with our prompt action, including the thoroughness of the AAR, but they were most pleased to see that the 'wrongdoer', as Ernie put it, had lost his privileges."

"Tell me how that's going," Mastone said.

"Not much to say. Newberry reduced Schlecter's privileges so that he can't operate alone. A senior surgeon observes his work on all cases. Because they don't have that many senior surgeons, Adam only gets to perform 2-3 cases a week. Newberry gets feedback on every case, and I hear from him once a week. Apparently, Adam is doing well under observation but is definitely chaffing under the restriction. He's making a lot of grumbling noises, complaining about things to the nurses and like that." Tim looked at Roslyn for affirmation of this last comment, but she shrugged her shoulders.

"What's next for him?" Sam wanted to know.

"Nothing's changed. The plan is still what I told you; he will continue to be observed with restricted privileges until Newberry thinks he can be re-instated."

"How long might that be?"

"I don't know. But I'm going to have another talk with Adam about adding the requirement that he recognizes his errors and quit blaming others."

Mastone nodded and said, "OK, then. Thanks, everyone," and started to rise from his chair.

Tom said, "Remember, I'll be out of the hospital today, over at the VA."

The nurses left along with Holly and Beverly, leaving Tom and Sam sitting at the table.

Sam looked at Tom for a moment, waiting for further explanation. When that didn't happen, he asked, "Why?"

"Do you know what day it is, Sam?"

"Uh, yes. It's Wednesday. Your usual day over there is Thursday, isn't it?"

"It's the 11th of November, Sam, Veterans Day. I'm the featured speaker at their ceremony."

"Oh yeah, right. I remember you told me about that."

"Lots of activity all over the country today. And every VA Medical Center will have special remembrance ceremonies and activities."

"Well, say hello to Bob for me," Sam said, referring to the Director of the VA Hospital. Sam smiled perfunctorily at Tom and went into his office.

Tom sat in his chair for another moment, thinking, "Mastone must not be very religious if he can't remember St. Veterans day!"

Chapter 13

The drive to the VA from New City was uneventful but as he entered the VA grounds, Tom noted the increase in traffic, both automobiles and foot traffic around the front entrance. Bob Summers, director of the hospital, had warned him that attendance at the Veterans Day ceremony would create a parking problem for the center and had encouraged him to use the offered valet parking.

Tom did not have the proclivity of flouting rank, preferring to be 'Doctor Bolling' when he attended at the VA, rather than 'General'. He used the usual visiting physician parking lot on those occasions even though Summers had offered him a spot in the dignitary lot. He did not intend to use the valet parking for the Veterans Day event, either. But he changed his mind when he saw the line of traffic the campus police were directing in the direction of the general parking. He quickly slipped the 'Valet' card Summers had sent him on the dash and turned into the drive up to the front entrance.

He was the third car in line, and he sat patiently watching as the first car, a specially equipped van, lowered its tailgate and hoist to allow the emergence of a man in a wheelchair wearing a familiar hat of the Veterans of Foreign Wars. The hoist deposited the man and chair on the ground, and an escort stepped behind the chair to wheel the veteran into the building. The van was driven away by one of the valets, and the driver accompanied his rider into the hospital.

The second car pulled up to the front, and the driver exited. She was a gray-haired lady carrying a small purse. As she walked around the car, another escort opened the passenger door and assisted a tall man to exit. As he did, Tom could see that the man was missing his right leg below the knee. The woman reached into the back seat of the car and retrieved a pair of crutches. With her assistance, the three individuals headed for the entrance. A valet driver jumped into the front seat and drove off.

Tom pulled up to the open spot and got out of his truck a little ashamedly. He left the keys in the ignition and smiled at the valet who came to move his vehicle. A young woman approached him as he walked around the front of the truck. She said, "Welcome, General. I'll escort you to Mr. Summers office. He wanted to see you when you arrived."

A little later, Tom was milling around in the auditorium crowd. He knew that the ceremony wasn't scheduled to start for another 15-20 minutes when he saw a familiar face.

"Hey, Razorback," he said, touching the other man on the shoulder.

Ron Looney turned, smiling at his friend. "Razor back at you," he said with a grin.

"I wondered if you'd be here," Tom said, shaking Ron's hand.

"I think that's the same thing you say to me every year."

"Could be. I wonder about you a lot."

"Well, I thought about taking a miss this year, and then I heard they had some VIP making the presentation this year, and I thought 'naw, I better go.' I might miss something."

"Yeah, you'd miss your invitation to the Christmas party, that's what."

"Oh, is there going to be a party?"

"Yes. Just like always. You can come if you promise to bring Meg."

"Consider it done. Assuming there will be a Petit Jean ham."

These two old friends shared a common bond of a career in the United States Air Force. Their careers were almost of two different eras but had a small overlap during which they met and formed a lasting friendship.

Ron was also from Arkansas, the son of a farmer outside the small southeastern town of Squashton. Like all such folks, Ron was a hunter, a fisherman, and an outdoorsman. He chose the military after high school and gravitated into the Security Police. While on active duty, he obtained special military training in investigations and earned a degree from Arizona State in Criminal Justice. His wife, Meg, was from Cincinnati, and that's where they moved when he retired. Meg's brother, a detective in Robbery with CPD, got him an interview. He ultimately was promoted to detective in the Homicide Division.

He and Tom met at Sheppard Air Force Base in Wichita Falls, Texas. Looney was a Master Sargent less than a year from retirement, and Tom was a recently minted Major in the medical corps right out of residency training. Tom had been sent to attend to a prisoner in the stockade, and Looney was the non-commissioned officer in charge. When the Major entered the building, someone shouted, 'Ten-hut. Officer in the building!' and everyone snapped to attention. The major stood transfixed until the MSgt whispered in his ear, 'As you were.'

The Major got the message and repeated the phrase loudly, and everyone went about their work. Tom frequently told that story on himself later, explaining he didn't know how to act when everyone stood on his entry into a room. Looney told Meg he thought Tom probably got used to that pretty soon after having a star on his shoulder.

Their subsequent friendship, built on a recognition of the unique Arkansas accent at first, was a part of Tom's decision to come to Cincinnati when he retired to take the position as chief of staff at New

City. Ron and Meg were regulars at Tom's Christmas party for the medical staff at New City, and Tom and Sandra were always part of Ron's fourth of July gathering with his police friends.

As they were catching up on family gossip, the escort from Summers' office appeared and said, "General, we are about to be seated." He patted Ron on the shoulder and moved to the side of the room, where he joined other speakers and Summers. Moments later, someone said, "Ten-hut," and the assembled guests stood. The rear door opened, and the flag bearers entered, following a drummer with his simple cadence. They carried the flag of the United States, Veterans Affairs, and the state of Ohio. Men in uniform saluted, others held their hands over their heart as the flags were marched to the front of the auditorium and up onto the stage. The march leader gave commands, and the bearers turned as one and slid their flagpoles into the waiting stands. Then they did a stomp-foot movement and stepped back two paces. Music came over the loud-speaker, and a woman stepped forward to a microphone on stage to sing the Star-Spangled Banner.

After the song, the salutes were smartly completed, and the speakers themselves moved onto the stage. Bob Summers stepped to the podium, and the official program began. Mr. Summers began by recognizing the veterans in the audience, then outlined the proceedings for the day. There were additional songs by staff, and a short, moving speech by the brother of a man who went missing in Afghanistan. When he finished speaking, the flag squad again marched in and placed the POW/MIA flag on the stage with the other flags. As they departed, the audience applauded. Bob Summers then introduced Tom Bolling, Brigadier General, United States Air Force Medical Corps, retired and currently the chief of staff at the New City Hospital.

Tom made the usual remarks about the role veterans have played in the nation's history. He began by re-introducing Colonel George Washington, chosen to lead the Continental Army in 1775. His point was that Colonel Washington was, at that time, a veteran of the French and Indian War. He mentioned others, including early leaders of the VA like General Omar Bradley, and he named current members of Congress who served in the military. Tom emphasized the importance of the G.I. Bill to America's recovery after World War II by funding educational benefits and insured home loans, two benefits that had influenced the American political, social, and economic interactions ever since. He drew on his orthopedic background to liken veterans and their service to the skeleton of a body. He forcefully noted how soft and useless that body would be without its bones or its veterans. And he reminded everyone that no one served 'alone'; they had brothers in arms, and their families back home supported them, as well. He said this day was for all who served, not just for those on the front lines and not just for those who came back home. He sat down to applause.

The rear doors opened again, and from there came the scree of a bagpipe. The player, adorned in the traditional kilt, Prince Charlie jacket with crossbelt, plaid cape, and a Black Watch Balmoral Tam. Slowly marching up to the front of the room, he played the poignant and lonely notes of 'Amazing Grace'. When he reached the front of the room, he turned and retraced his steps, playing all the way. The platform speakers stepped down and filed behind him, signifying that the program was over.

CHAPTER 14

Adam Schlecter almost bounced as he entered the laboratory that morning. He grinned and made pleasantries with both Bonnie and Terry. After his coat was deposited in the little office area, he went to the changing area and shortly came back out, all garbed in scrubs and booties, eager to talk with the others.

According to Adam, he had been downcast for the past few months and had centered his thinking on the onus that had been put on him by the operative death. He realized that he had spent all his time thinking only about his surgical activity, he said. But he started thinking more about the research in the last week, and now he felt he had a breakthrough thought.

"I realized that I've been thinking rather linearly," he said.

Bonnie and Terry were aware that Schlecter was a believer in the realms of complexity and chaos and that many problems were not 'linear' and could not be solved with linear thinking.

"I've been stuck with the idea that we had to have one size bubble with only one porosity in the implants," he said excitedly. He looked at the two technicians expectantly. Bonnie nodded, and Terry dropped his head.

"Well," Adam continued, "what if we don't do that? What happens then?"

"I don't understand," Bonnie said.

Terry looked at Adam from under his eyebrows.

"I think that if we wanted a curve with early rapid diffusion of content from the bubbles like if we wanted to have a quick high curve followed by a low steady one, we would have to have two balloon implants, you know, one with high permeability and the other with low permeability, right?"

They both nodded.

"But this liposome thing makes such a difference. We can make solutions with liposomes that diffuse slowly and others that diffuse more quickly, and we can mix them in the same balloon. See?"

Bonnie slowly nodded. Terry moved his head a little, thinking to himself that the idea Schlecter was expounding was almost exactly what he, Terry, had suggested to the researcher over a month previously.

Terry had been quite excited when he determined that he could predictably produce antibiotic liposomes with predictable diffusion indices even across variable porosity balloon membranes. He actually spent most of one weekend in the laboratory just writing the potential for these results in his logbook. He had brought the idea to Schlecter after a particularly unenergetic Monday meeting. Adam hadn't really listened to him, and Terry decided to explain his thoughts later. He was frankly put out that Adam Schlecter thought this great idea was his own. But he didn't say anything and actually made additional suggestions about the practical aspect of implementing the concept.

Schlecter spent the entire day in the laboratory. He was active and engaged in his own development of membranes with stable porosity and long life after implantation. His most recent idea was to impair the body's capability to resorb the balloon after implantation. To accomplish this, his most recent idea involved treating the membranes with a dilute solution of formaldehyde for varying periods of time before bubble formation.

He walked around the lab while experiments were underway and looked over the technicians' shoulders to see how their work was progressing. He made comments and gave some suggestions and encouragement and, unusual for him, praise.

At the end of the day, Bonnie prepared to leave but stuck around longer than usual because the boss was still working. Schlecter had even changed scrubs and seemed just as active as if the day was just beginning. Terry wanted to leave but took his cue from Bonnie and hung around. Neither of them started any project that would take hours to finish, however, and Adam finally tumbled to it.

"Go on, you guys. It's getting dark. Get out of those scrubs and go home. I'm just kinda enthused here and want to finish this."

Neither of them took a second urging. Bonnie quickly changed back into her street clothes and headed out. They walked into the parking lot together.

"What do you think is going on?" Terry asked

"What do you mean?"

"I mean, after two months of him moping around and we couldn't get direction from him with a can opener, and now he's the 'Jolly Researcher'."

"Well, first of all, he's had a tough go of it recently, with that operative death and his privileges cut back. Plus, I've seen this almost manic behavior in the past when he gets on to an idea. And, perhaps most importantly, we got a lot done today, and this may not last. So. Let's be glad we've got our guy back and keep on keeping on."

Terry nodded. "Yep, it was a good day. Let's hope it continues tomorrow."

"By the way," Bonnie said, "you shouldn't be wearing your scrubs home. The whole point of having them in the lab is for cleanliness."

"I know. I change into new ones every morning."

"That's not the point."

"Yeah, I hear you." Terry looked up at the unlit parking lot lights. "I'll walk you to your car. It's dark out here."

CHAPTER 15

Tuesday, December 22

Taking a piece of his military background with him into civilian life, Tom Bolling always held a large Christmas Party for his direct reports in the week before The Day. The military custom was for the commanding officer of a base to hold a Christmas Holiday Party with what was understood to be mandatory attendance. Special occasions in the military often called for special dress. In the Air Force, that uniform is called the Mess Dress, and the functions for which that uniform is required are called 'dining in' or dining out'. The difference is that 'dining in' affairs are for military unit members only. The Commander's Christmas Holiday Party was considered a Dining Out, and spouses were included.

Commanders' parties did not hold to the same rules as a 'dining out', however. Attendees at dining in or dining out functions were expected to stay for the duration. The Holiday Parties, on the other hand, were 'drop-in' affairs. Officers were there to be seen and then to get out of the way. Tom liked the party idea but did not want to have either Mess Dress uniforms or 'drop-in, drop-out' as the protocol. He and Sandra arranged a specific time for their party with beginning and ending times noted on the invitations.

Nonetheless, when he held his first party at New City, someone looked up military protocol and passed the word that this was a 'must show' affair but could easily be 'drop in and drop out' so attendees could get to another party or anywhere else. But after they showed up at the party, most found that they weren't too eager to leave.

First, there was the food. Sandra Bolling laid out a smorgasbord of fine eats to appeal to everyone. There were various kinds of hors d'oeurves, cheeses with paired crackers, hot and cold dips, plus bowls of assorted nuts and some fruit. And there were desserts in every room of the house; homemade rum cake, pecan pies, chocolate cake, brownies, and a wide assortment of cookies.

Unlike the military parties of note, there was no Grog Bowl. Tom offered guests a drink choice: wine, red or white, or non-alcoholic drinks ranging from sodas, lemonade, coffee, hot or iced tea, mulled cider to what Sam Newberry called 'diet water', unsweetened flavored water. If someone chose wine, Tom would pour their first glass and tell them they were on their own thereafter.

But universally, the center of attention for all returnees was the large spiral-sliced peppered ham from Petit Jean Meats in Arkansas. Sandra always arrayed biscuits, rolls, crackers, and pita slices to handle the ham. And, of course, to dress the ham on the bread of choice, there were several condiments to appeal to any taste, two German mustards, one spicy and one Dijon-flavored, real mayonnaise and Tom's homemade horseradish-in-whipped cream dressing.

In the early years of the party, some surgical staff had not attended because they had difficulty finding sitters for their children. The Bollings adapted by outfitting a children's room for the party, compatible with almost all ages. There were children's snacks, comfortable seating, DVDs of favorite Christmas movies, and games for them to play. Over time, the children showed they favored the ham and the brined shrimp as much as did the adults.

The Bolling's home was not huge, but it was designed for entertaining with no dead ends. Each room had, in addition to the various cakes and desserts, plenty of seating. People came and stayed and left only after talking to others they had not seen for conversation in weeks. Plenty of room for seating existed throughout the house, but the dining room usually was crowded. That was especially true around the ham and whipped cream end of the table.

The Looney's were fixtures at this party and functioned almost as second hosts. Many hospital personnel had met Ron during some recent events at the hospital, and others wanted to meet him because of what they had heard. In their role as 'hosts', the Looney's always came early to assist the preparation and layout if necessary. Sandra was happy to have Meg's assistance in the kitchen, but Ron usually found that Tom had everything else handled.

They usually joked with each other about the Arkansas ham, Ron insisting it should be 'taste tested' before allowing guests to partake. Tom noted that, unlike the earlier years, there were now several 'taste experts' on the staff. They did not need a 'tester'.

But even all the logistics and management that went into the purchasing and preparing of food and cleaning of the house and decorating it for Christmas paled in comparison to the wisdom and cleverness Sandra Bolling employed when she sent out invitations. She realized that a civilian party did not have the military 'drop in and drop out' tradition. And, she knew even the large house would not hold everyone all night. So, she crafted the invitation announcement as having a distinct 'start' and 'stop' time. Everyone took the hint, and within twenty minutes of the first person saying, "Well, we should get going," everyone had collected his or her coat and said their goodbyes.

And then the pair of hosts started the cleanup. Ron and Tom circled the house, picking up glasses and dishes for washing, and Sandra and Meg took on the task of apportioning food for storing, freezing, or sharing. Before long, the two Arkansas guys sat in the cleaned living room, clinking longneck beer bottles and talking over their respective professional troubles.

"That was a good presentation you made on Veterans Day," Ron said, tilting his bottle toward Tom in an unofficial salute.

"Thanks. It's one of those things that continues to bug me at New City, the lack of understanding of the VA and its mission."

"Well, they didn't serve."

"Actually, some did. It's not them. It's management, like Sam Mastone. He forgot what day it was."

"Is that why you look troubled?"

"Do I? Look troubled? What's that look like anyway?"

"Your eyebrows are pinched together, even when you're smiling."

"Yeah, well, I am troubled. Thanks for noticing. Now I have to tell you what's going on, right?"

"That's the way it works."

Tom smiled wryly, then stared over Ron's head for few seconds before starting to talk. "You know about the Joint Commission, right?"

"That's the Chicago group that says you're OK or not, right?"

"Close enough. In fact, that's spot on. The Joint, as we call 'em, got all over us a couple of years ago."

"I remember. You pulled the AAR out of the hat and got them off your back."

"That's certainly the way I'd like for things to have gone. But they still had this 'black mark' on our record. They could decide to have another site visit at any time."

"Sounds like the IG. But you're all ready for them, right?" Ron nodded to himself as he took a drink from his bottle. "I mean, you said there was only one thing they dinged you for, and you fixed it."

"Again, that's what I would like to believe. The truth is, everybody spends months getting ready for a site visit from the Joint. Usually, that is a waste of time. But hospital people are afraid of a visit when they don't have time to prepare. A surprise visit gives no time for preparation and that causes anxiety. Trouble. And, we may be facing a surprise visit."

"Is that it? You're worried about a surprise visit that you think you're ready for?"

"No. We had a major event couple of months back. Intra-operative death."

Ron whistled his sympathy.

"I reported it. Did another AAR. Took action. Did all the right things. But I'm still troubled, as you say."

"Why?"

"The action I took was to restrict the privileges of the surgeon in charge. He's taking the reduction very poorly, and I can't see any way to put him back to full privileges if he doesn't admit he was wrong."

"What's this Joint say?"

"I talked to a friend, former Army Colonel, now their VP for Accreditation. He tells me that we are 'back to an even keel' again. Odd language for an Army guy. But, he also says they have a general concern about New City because of 'all the trouble with homicides'."

"What trouble? You had 'em, and I caught 'em. End of story." Ron pointed his beer bottle at Tom to make the point.

"Not the way the Joint sees it. There must be something going on at New City to foster 'all those homicides', or at least they think so."

"Are there more?

"More what?"

"More homicides.

"No. The operative death was negligence. We paid out a ton of money to the family. Young woman, mother of two."

"Geez. I'm sorry."

"So, I'm troubled. If we have any more big events, Mastone may give me some walking papers," Tom said with a big sigh.

"Fire you?" Ron sat up straight.

"Yes."

"Can he do that?" Ron asked, leaning forward.

"Yes."

"Then what would you do?"

"I'd have to look for a job; maybe move."

"Now I'm troubled."

Chapter 16

Thursday, January 7

Tom and Beverly left the morning meeting and walked back toward their offices. Beverly Hancock had been an important part of helping Tom adjust to the civilian attitudes and interdepartmental strife at New City from the moment he arrived. One of Tom's major goals was to teach process improvement methods to the medical staff. Another was to get their commitment to teaching those concepts to their staff. He had already had some successes in reducing waiting times in both specialty and primary care clinics and had done some good teaching on the subject.

Bev was an experienced administrator with several years of experience with New City politics. She also knew the history of certain policy decisions. She had read Deming's book, *Out of the Crisis,* and, like Tom, believed there was some application to medical care of manufacturing concepts about performance improvement. Tom knew that Bev was a vital and indispensable part of his successes so far. Her ability to analyze situations, obtain and share critical data and recommend courses of action based on knowledge of personalities had kept Tom from making several blunders in the first couple of years. Tom thought Bev must share a 'hive mind' with his wife because the two of them would often offer the same general advice on specific topics.

They noticed one of the staff physicians standing at Mary's desk. He looked up as they approached and somewhat tersely nodded at Bev and said, "Tom, can we talk?"

"Of course, Burton, come on in." Tom indicated his office as Bev turned toward hers. She looked at Mary for an indication of the issue, but Mary just shrugged her shoulders.

"Have a seat, Burton," Tom said, leading the way into his office.

"No need. I'm just here to complain."

"You look pretty upset about something. What's going on?"

"I don't know where Adam Schlecter is."

"Uh-huh. And why is that your concern?"

"Sam's asked me to monitor him in the operating room a couple of times a week, and I pushed some things around on my schedule to do that."

"Right. Sam's been keeping me apprised of your reports."

"Well, he didn't show for a scheduled first case today."

"Adam?"

"Yes. He scheduled this case a week ago, and I had to move something around to be here, and then he doesn't show. And he didn't tell me or the patient or anybody."

"Has someone tried to find him?"

Very exasperated at the line of questioning, Burton said, "Yes, Tom. We have all tried calling him. On his cell and at home and in the lab and all that. He isn't answering any calls, and I don't know where he is, and I'm getting pretty upset about this pampering that's going on."

"Hold on," Tom said. "What happened to the patient?"

"I canceled the surgery when Schlecter didn't show after 30 minutes. She's pretty angry, too."

"Have you talked to Sam?"

"Of course. I called him when Adam didn't answer his cell phone. He's the one that gave me the home phone number to call. He knows about it."

"All right, Burton. I hear you. Just calm down, please. I don't know what's going on, either. But I agree this is pretty disturbing behavior. I'll take it from here. You get back to the Operating Room. Tell everyone that I'm looking into the issue and that I'll let them know what's going on today."

"What are you going to tell them?" Burton asked, not moving toward the door.

"I will tell them, and you, whatever I find out when I find it out."

"Well, what do you think would make him do this?"

"Look, Burton, I don't know, and I'm not about to speculate. I'll just go find out. And then I'll let you know. Got it?" Tom's voice and body language as he stood up from behind his desk was a clear indication that the conversation was over. Burton was not slow about picking up on the hint and said, "OK, then. Later it is." And he left the office.

Tom sat down again and buzzed Bev in her office. She came right away, and they discussed options. Tom called Sam Newberry's office asked his secretary to find him and ask him to come to Tom's office.

Bev asked, "What do you think?"

"I don't have a clue. Would you have Mary call Adam's cell phone and his home for me? And then I want you to get his personnel folder and see if there are any other family members in the area."

Bev nodded and headed out the door, almost colliding with Sam Newberry who looked at Tom and commented, "Don't look to me for answers. I've already called all the places I know he could be. I bet he's had a wreck or something."

"Possibly," Tom agreed. "But until we know his actual whereabouts I'm going to go looking. Come with me."

He headed for the Research wing with Sam trailing behind. Tom asked over his shoulder, "Have there been any incidents in the Operating Room that you know of?"

"No. I'm telling you every week what's been going on, and he is actually doing better. No absence periods and no judgment errors."

"Any other idea what might have set him off? Anybody making fun of his mentorship? Cracks about his capability or anything like that?"

"C'mon, Tom. I would have said so if I knew anything like that. I have no idea what might have run him off the rails."

At the laboratory entrance, Tom opened the door and saw Bonnie leaning over a set of vessels. She heard the door open and partially turned toward the sound.

"Oh, Dr. Bolling. I thought you were Dr. Schlecter."

"Has he been here this morning?"

"Oh no. He had surgery this morning. First case, I think. So I thought he might be through by now."

"Have you heard anything from him this morning? Anything at all? A call, text?"

"No, sir," she replied, setting her work down and giving Tom and Sam her complete attention. "Is something wrong?"

"He didn't show for surgery, and we're looking for him to find out why."

"No, sir. We have had no contact today," she indicated Terry, who had come up during the conversation. He nodded his agreement with the statement.

Tom turned to Sam and said, "I'm going to his house. Do you want to come with me?"

CHAPTER 17

Thursday, January 7

They rode mostly in silence to Schlecter's home. Tom drove his F-150, and Sam Newberry sat quietly in the passenger seat. The atmosphere was tense, and conversation between them was forced, but they both played it professionally.

"You ever been here?" Tom asked as they entered the neighborhood.

"No," Sam replied. "Never had cause."

"He and his wife didn't come to the Christmas Party."

"Anne."

"And what?"

"Anne. Her name is Anne."

"Oh, right. I haven't seen her in quite a while."

Sam nodded agreement as Tom pulled into the Schlecter's driveway. He parked right behind Adam's Mercedes E350 and remembered the day Adam had purchased the car and told everyone about it. High-performance engine, leather seats, all the accessories like seat warmers and backup camera. He was really proud of the car, Tom remembered. He put his hand on the hood, shook his head, and said to Newberry, "Cold."

The house itself seemed cold as they gained the porch; no lights and no movement. Tom rang the doorbell and got no answer. He knocked vigorously and the door jarred open. It had not been securely closed and was not locked. The two physicians looked at each other and hesitated. Then Tom said, "I have a friend in the police department who says, it's not breaking and entering if the door isn't locked."

"Still . . ."

"Plus, he says there's an obligation to enter if there's a possibility of someone needing help."

'Well, you go first," said the chairman of surgery.

Inside the house, they noticed the lack of lights again, making some of the interior seem unnecessarily dark. They quickly realized there was no one on the first floor. Tom stood at the bottom of the stairs and listened.

"I think I hear someone up there," he said quietly to Newberry.

He received a nod of agreement and then said, more loudly, "Adam. Are you up there?"

Faintly they heard a voice. "G'way."

Instead, encouraged that their colleague was apparently upstairs they both hurried up.

"Adam, it's Tom and Sam Newberry. Where are you?"

"G'way," came from a front bedroom, and they went in there and saw Adam sitting in a chair beside a hospital bed. In the bed, Anne Schlecter, obviously dead, lay facing upward, looking very wasted, her face drawn and her hair thinned appreciably. She had a nasal cannula in place connected to a running oxygen concentrator at the bedside. The room was cluttered with other implements of care for the bedridden, stacks of bedside medications, a bedside commode, and boxes of bed pads and other medical supplies. The bedside tabletop was strewn with bottles and drink containers and facial tissues.

Tom and Newberry stopped in their tracks for a moment to take in the meaning of the setting. Then Tom stepped toward Adam and said, "C'mon Adam, let's get a cup of coffee." He reached out his hand to help Schlecter to his feet but got no response for several seconds. Then Adam looked slowly up at Tom and said, "She's dead."

"Yes. I can see that. We can talk about it over a cup of coffee. Let's go." Again he held out his hand. This time Schlecter put his hand in Tom's and allowed himself to be pulled to a standing position.

"When did she die, Adam?" Tom asked, putting an arm around Schlecter.

After another several second pause, Adam said, softly, "This morning. Early. I've been sitting here ever since just . . ."

"She's obviously been sick a long time," Tom observed.

"Ovarian cancer. She's been in hospice for the past seven weeks."

"I'm so sorry, Adam. I had no idea." Tom began walking Adam toward the stairs. Newberry moved out of the way and then followed them down into the kitchen. At the table, Newberry sat next to Schlecter and placed his hand on Adam's arm. "You said she was in hospice?"

"Yeah," he said dispiritedly. He turned his reddened eyes to Newberry. "Why?'

"Well, hospice organizations ask you to call them when the death occurs. They will take care of things. Have you called them, Adam?"

"No. I didn't want to disturb anyone. I just sat there beside her."

"If you will tell me where the stuff is that the hospice people left for you, I'll make the call."

"Uh, I don't remember. Probably somewhere in the bedroom. I don't want to lose her." As he said this, Adam's eye wet up and he began to cry.

Struck by this plaint, Tom and Newberry stopped for a moment, and then Tom indicated that Newberry should go back upstairs and said to Adam, "Look, this call has to be made, you know that, don't you?" When Adam nodded, Newberry left and, Tom asked, "Where do you keep the coffee?" His intent to distract Schlecter apparently worked as Adam began pointing at various cabinets to locate the coffee, the cups, and the sweeteners.

Not much later, Tom was putting a cup of strong coffee in front of Adam as Newberry re-entered. "They're on the way. We will stay to make sure things are sorted out, Adam. If that's all right with you."

Schlecter looked up at them both and nodded, then took a sip of his coffee, set the cup down, and leaned back in his chair with tears streaming down his face.

The hospice personnel did as they had promised. They were very professional with their solicitous care for Adam and Anne. They removed the body and left information with Adam about the funeral home. Over the next hour, other team members appeared and removed the oxygen concentrator, the hospital bed, and other items. Tom called Mary in his office to let her know the situation and asked her to notify Sam Mastone.

Sam Newberry thought it necessary to let the surgical service staff know what had happened, and he left while the hospice people were finishing their dismantling of the care area. Tom sat with Adam and slowly drew out the story of Anne's diagnosis back in the previous summer. She had metastases throughout the abdomen at diagnosis and did not respond to initial courses of chemotherapy. In fact, she developed significant side effects and elected to stop treatment right after Thanksgiving.

Tom thought back to when he and Newberry had been dealing with Schlecter's surgical shortcomings without realizing what Adam was dealing with in his private life. He wondered why it had never occurred to him to ask, "Adam is everything all right at home?" He was aware that Alan, the son, had left home during that time, and now there seemed to be a reason for that, but he didn't ask about anything else. He sat there mostly silent with Adam, provided him more coffee, and found him something to eat.

Finally, Tom asked, "Adam do you have other family I could call? Or friends to come and stay with you tonight?" He received a slow shake of the head to each query. "What are you going to do?"

"I'm going to the funeral home and set things up. Then I will come home and probably get the first night of straight through sleep in the last two months."

CHAPTER 18

Saturday, January 9

Everyone was surprised that Anne's funeral was held so soon after her death. Adam explained that neither she nor he had any family to come so there was no reason to wait. They did not know where Alan was to notify him and had relied solely on the death notice in the newspaper.

At the graveside, there were less than a dozen mourners. The minister commented about the brevity and uncertainty of life on this earth but spoke encouraging words to Adam about Anne and the life hereafter. Adam sat immobile at the graveside as if he didn't hear the ceremony. After a final prayer, the minister shook Adam's hand, and that seemed to bring Adam back into the world. He smiled and nodded to the minister and others as they slowly passed by him and offered condolence.

Then it was just Adam, Tom, and Sandra anywhere around. Adam gave up the play-acting of a brave front and slumped in the chair. Tom went to him and suggested they go get something to eat. Adam sat still for a moment and then nodded and got up. He looked at the casket one last time and walked with Tom to a waiting car. The funeral director had remained behind to offer Adam a ride back to the funeral home but Tom indicated that he would see that Adam got there to pick up his car.

Tom and Sandra drove Adam to a well-known diner nearby and settled in for a discussion and meal. Even though it was nearly noon, all three decided they would have breakfast. Once they placed their orders, Tom said, "Adam, I've talked with Sam Newberry. We both think it would do you some good right now to take a little sabbatical. What do you think?"

"You mean stop doing surgery altogether?"

"For a while, yes. But we thought that maybe you would like to go somewhere for some study and collaboration about your research."

"Really?"

"Yes, really. You know that's what a sabbatical is really about, taking time away from duties to gain additional knowledge."

"Well, yeah, I guess I did know that."

"Are there other labs working in your field where you could spend some time?"

"I don't know. There's one place in Los Angeles that's working on something like what I'm doing with the membrane and all, but I'm ahead of them. I'd be teaching my competition to go out there."

Tom sat quietly for a moment, waiting to see if Adam picked up on the conversation. He was about to when their orders came, and for the next 15 minutes talking at the table was kept to a minimum and mostly involved passing salt and pepper shakers or cream for the coffee.

As everyone finished with their meal, Sandra gave Tom a look from under her eyebrows, and he spoke to Adam, "Well, maybe you'd want to spend the sabbatical here in your own lab. That would give you time to get at some of those things you talked about at the research conference."

Adam seemed a little encouraged by that idea. "There are some things I haven't tried yet," he said. "But no surgery?"

Tom said as soothingly as he could, "Look, Adam, let's do one thing at a time, OK? If you want to stay here for a sabbatical away from the operating room to focus on your research, Newberry and I will back it. When you get the primary research done and can hand it over to the technicians in your lab, we will talk about surgical privileges, I promise."

Adam's smile was tight, but he nodded and signaled for another cup of coffee. Tom went on, "Besides, if you're going to be around and on the grounds, I think it would be a good idea for you to get some counseling about depression."

"I'm not depressed."

"Well, if you're not, you are missing some of the most powerful reasons to be depressed."

"I'm not depressed."

"You certainly are fooling a lot of us around the hospital, then, because you are certainly acting like you're depressed. You didn't finish your food right there in front of you."

"Look, I'm not depressed. I'm just sad. Really sad. Anne and I had plans to travel after Alan left home. I mean, when he went to college. Everything about my life seems to be circling the drain right now."

"That's a good reason for counseling. Even if you are not depressed."

After a brief pause, Adam picked up his cup and drained it. "I'll think about it, OK? Now can we go get my car?"

CHAPTER 19

Tuesday, February 16

Bonnie looked across the laboratory at Terry and noticed how slowly he was working. She recognized the step in his preparation that was holding his concentration. She put her work aside for a minute. She walked over to his area and watched as he moved the three-liter container of ethanol containing the mixture of dissolved lipids and antibiotics to the end of the counter-top. He had been slowly introducing the materials into the container until they reached the appropriate concentration. Bonnie enjoyed the visual changes that accompanied the next steps in Terry's work. She leaned against the counter and grinned at him when he looked up and noticed her standing nearby.

"Wanna learn how to do this?" he asked, smiling at her.

"Oh no, you're the expert. I want to see the pretty picture it makes."

"Yeah, I know," he said as he adjusted the settings on a thick glass-walled chamber into which he volumetrically placed 50 milliliters of the solvent. Bonnie watched as he closed the gasket top and tightened all the corner thumbscrews.

"I figured out the settings to adjust the liposome size," Terry said while he inserted the sonicator into the top of the chamber and then placed the whole apparatus into an ice bath. He moved the ice bath to the edge of the counter-top, saying, "I know you like to watch the formation."

Bonnie slid over to the counter and looked down into the clear liquid in the chamber, and said, "I'm ready."

Terry adjusted the settings on the sonicator and turned it on. Immediately, Bonnie could feel the vibration in the counter and the chamber. She watched with some pleasure as the small tail of iridescence began to form around the sonicator probe. Terry had placed the chamber on a magnetic mixer and now turned that on at a low speed. The result was the iridescent tail of liposomes began to spin away from the probe and form a whirl of vacillating light ranging from light blue to pink. Bonnie watched in fascination, almost hypnotized by the whirling light show.

When Terry's timer went off, he stopped the sonicator but let the stirrer continue to run for another minute. Bonnie looked up and smiled at him. "Thanks," she said. "I really like that. What were you making?"

"That's a batch of mostly 20-nanometer liposomes containing aqueous penicillin. I still have to filter them to get the bigger ones out, and then I'll store them in the refrigerator until I have all the sizes we need for the animal experiments."

"Has he said anything to you about when we can start working with the animals again?"

"No. I was down in the cage area last week. I asked Scotty if Schlecter had ordered any more rabbits. He hadn't. So, we keep on making these things and wait."

"Well, I've pretty much settled the process for changing the bubble permeability, so . . ."

"And I certainly have this process working right. We need to ask him about moving into the animals."

"He's sitting back there, staring at the wall. Let's go ask him."

"You go. You're the senior one here. I need to get these 'somes into storage.

Bonnie looked toward the rear of the laboratory and then back at Terry. He just cocked his head at her and went to work on opening the sonic chamber. Bonnie took a deep breath and went to see Schlecter.

"Doctor?" she said at the entrance to his small office area.

"Hmm. What?" he said distractedly.

"Terry and I are up to speed on membrane and liposome prep. We think we are ready for the next phase of animal testing."

"Huh. Well, yeah. That's good, I guess. Better late . . ."

"Shall I ask Scotty to get us some rabbits?"

"Uh . . .probably not. I need to tell you guys something. Let me meet you out there in a minute."

Bonnie frowned at him but nodded and moved back into the laboratory. Schlecter didn't move from his desk. She went back to Terry's area and said, "He's coming out with some information. It doesn't look good."

Terry also frowned but continued draining the liquid from the chamber into a labeled flask. Making a face at Bonnie, he went into the walk-in refrigerator and shelved the flask. When he came back, she was still standing at his work area. Terry pulled off his surgical gloves and leaned against the opposite counter with his arms folded. "Did he say when?"

"Apparently, right now," she said, indicating with a nod of her head in the direction of the office area.

Schlecter slouched over to where they were standing. His head made a circular motion allowing him to look at each of them in passing, but then he looked at the ceiling and said, "Mac just told me we are under early review."

"Why?" asked Bonnie. "We have approval for another what, year or so?"

"Budget cuts," Schlecter said tersely. "They are reviewing projects early that have not made progress reports since last review indicating successful advancement."

"That's not fair," said Terry. We haven't been able to get to the animal phase yet."

"I know," Schlecter said. "It's not certain that we will lose funding, but we needed to have some progress reported to be sure of continuation."

"Can we submit what we've accomplished with the membranes and the liposomes?" Bonnie asked. "We have some real progress there."

"Apparently, they are only looking at progress reports submitted by the first of the year."

"Well, when will we hear?"

"I don't really know. A month or so, I'd guess. Not enough time to get any significant animal work done. And it likely wouldn't count anyway."

"What do you want us to do, then?"

"Make sure your processes work and get the documentation complete."

They looked at each other in silence for a minute and then returned to their own area, Schlecter back to his office.

Terry soon migrated over to Bonnie's area and, "This is really crappy. I was hoping for a good recommendation from him to get into medical school. What happens if he loses the funding?"

"We don't have jobs, that's what. Maybe we can find something else here in the city. I don't know. And you're absolutely right. This is Grade A crappy!"

Chapter 20

Bonnie looked up from the area where she was working on the documentation of her processes. She got Terry's attention and asked, "Are you applying to South West Ohio Medical School?"

Terry nodded and then answered, "Sure, it's the school right here in town. No traveling and no change of address cards."

"Well, you wouldn't have to worry about finding a job then. Going to Med School is a big enough job."

"Still gonna have to pay for it and live in the meantime."

"You applying for next year?"

"Uh-huh."

"You're going to hear soon, then. Right?"

"Should be in the next few days."

"Good luck. Have you applied for scholarships or loans?"

"All depends on having the letter of acceptance. Have you thought about what you would do?"

"A little. There's no opening for my skills here or at the medical school or the VA. I looked. I probably could learn something new, but I'm kinda mid-career. I actually called Fender's lab to see if they need help."

"Really? That's L.A. Long ways off. What did Schlecter say? He and Fender fight about stuff all the time."

"I didn't tell him I called. And don't you, either. I don't want any hard feelings if our funding is continued."

"If we can just get to the animal phase, I'm pretty sure these new 'somes are gonna be the answer."

"Only because the new membranes I developed will let them do their job," she smiled.

"Right. Right. Let's hope we get to find out."

Shortly after that, Terry got up and stretched and said, "I'm done. Going home. Gotta get some groceries." He grabbed his coat from the rack by the door and opened the door.

"Wait a minute," Bonnie said. "Didn't we talk about not wearing your scrubs home after work?"

"Yes, we did," Terry allowed with a grin. "I just didn't agree with you." He walked out, and the door closed behind him.

CHAPTER 21

Monday, March 15

A month had now passed without any further word on funding, and Schlecter had seemed more upbeat each day. Bonnie was early into the lab, preparing for the usual Monday mid-morning meeting. She and Terry had finished their updates on all documentation the previous week, and she thought they could start doing some additional *in vitro* studies to show the efficacy of the new membranes. She planned to bring that up at the meeting and try to get Schlecter enthused about it.

She hung up her coat on the rack and looked around. Clearly, she was first in the laboratory that morning. There was a small one-cup coffee brewer in a corner, and she made herself a quick cup and set about to get things ready for the meeting. There would be no point in waiting for mid-morning since there was no activity in the lab that needed to be put on 'pause'.

Just then, Adam Schlecter entered the lab and called out to her, "Beat me in this morning, I see."

"Not by much. I barely got my coffee made. Want me to make you a cup?"

"No, thanks. I'm going to run over to the Green Bean in a minute. I want something special."

"Can we have the meeting when you get back?"

"Absolutely. Where's Terry?"

"He'll be here, I'm sure."

Schlecter went back to his office area, hung up his coat, and put his briefcase on the desk. He sat down and made a phone call, then walked back toward the door.

"Terry back yet?"

"No, sir. Are you going for coffee now?"

"Yep. Won't be long. I have something I want to discuss with both of you when I get back."

"Heard about the funding?"

"Ah, no. I just think we should be doing something and not sitting around; I've got some ideas, you know."

"I agree. And I have some ideas, too."

"Good. Back soon, then." Schlecter left on his way to the lobby.

Less than ten minutes later, Terry came in wearing the same scrubs he had on when he left. He was not wearing a coat or hat and went quietly to his area and sat down, slumped in his chair. Bonnie almost missed his entrance but caught sight of him at his desk and called out, "The boss was just here. He's gone for coffee, but he wants to meet when he returns."

The only reaction from Terry was a dispirited nod.

Bonnie started to say something else to him but was interrupted by a blustery entrance into the lab by Alston MacFarlane, the Research Director at New City. 'Mac' as he was known, was completely Scottish in looks and dress. He was a stocky man about five foot eight inches, burly in the chest, and walked with a rolling gait. His head was large and made even larger by his thick, golden-red full-face beard and longish haircut. Green eyes showed out from under bushy eyebrows and were usually sparkling with humor and wit. Now, however, his eyes were neither jovial nor friendly. He saw Bonnie and brusquely asked, "Where's Schlecter?"

"He went for coffee, Dr. Mac. Can I give him a message when he comes back?"

"Oh, no. Thank you, m'dear. This'll have to come from me. Where did he go?"

"To the Green Bean, he said. He'll be right back. Want to wait?"

"No. I can't. But you need to know about it, too. The Institute just informed me that they are rescinding the funding from Adam's work as of now. He's going to be so disappointed."

"Wait. Does that mean we can't keep up with our research?"

"That's exactly what it means, dearie. I'm sorry, but this lab is now closed. You'll get some severance, I'm sure. We always do that. But there's no more research, and all funding is being pulled back."

"We were afraid of this," she said, looking over at Terry who did not seem to be paying attention. He was staring into space and crumpling a piece of paper.

"I've got to find Adam," MacFarlane said. "Green Bean, eh? Fancy stuff, that." He turned and left the laboratory without further comment. Bonnie stood and watched him for a moment and then took a deep breath and sighed it out. "Well, Terry, now we have the reality to live with, eh?"

Terry got up from his desk and walked out the door without a word. Bonnie watched him go, as well. Then, thinking to herself, 'You ain't alone, boyo. Schlecter will probably throw something and break glassware.'

As she thought that, she got up and started cleaning up the laboratory of glassware and putting machinery and equipment back into cabinets.

CHAPTER 22

Mastone entered the conference room promptly at eight o'clock with the daily reports in his hand. He took his seat at the head of the conference table and looked around the room. "Everything was quiet last night, I see. No issues." He looked at Tom and then at Roslyn to see if they had topics to discuss.

Roslyn said, "The broken window in the outpatient clinic has not been repaired."

Sam looked at Holly, who bent over her notepad and scribbled.

"It's cold in those rooms," Roslyn said as if she expected that someone would disagree with her.

Sam nodded and turned to Tom.

After a short period of looking at each other, Tom said without inflection, "I know a guy who repairs windows."

Mastone replied, "So do I. He works for me."

"Oh," said Tom, raising his eyebrows.

"Hmmph!" said Roslyn.

"I will have him down there today, Roslyn, I promise," Mastone said. "Anything else?"

Tom said, "We had another return to the operating room yesterday. Not completely unexpected. Not a reportable case."

"Good," Mastone sighed. "The last thing we need is another Sentinel Event. And, by the way, have you paved that over with the Joint Commission?"

Tom nodded slightly and he explained, "Yes, mostly. They want to see the completion of our plan of rehabilitation for Schlecter. The Board was pleased with our 'timely and thorough' approach. Tom used his fingers to mimic quotation marks.

"That sounds good," Sam said.

Everyone agreed by nodding, including Holly.

"Well, I'm quoting my old friend, their vice president of accreditation," Tom explained. "He says things will likely fade away from everyone's concern in another few months."

"By the way," Mastone asked, "What about Schlecter?" I understand he went missing."

"Well, he lost his funding for his research. He hasn't come in the hospital all week. But I don't know that he's missing," Tom said.

"I understand he stormed out of the hospital and didn't come back."

"Yes, that's right."

"Well, what's going on with him?"

Tom took a deep breath and said, "You recall that Newberry and I restricted his privileges, so he wasn't doing much surgery. Then we found out his wife died, and we put him on a research sabbatical from the operating room."

"What does that mean, a 'research sabbatical'?"

"We moved his salary from the surgical service to the research service and gave him six months to bring his research to the next level. We planned to move him back to the operating room with supervision in stages."

"So, what's happening now that his NIH funding is gone?" Sam cut to the heart of the matter.

"Sam Newberry and I have talked about it. We were giving him this week to calm down. We plan to move his return to the operating room up on the schedule and start his rehabilitation next week."

"Will that work?"

"We think so. He's a good surgeon who has had a lot of pressure on him recently. Besides, he no longer has a salary unless he gets back in the operating room. I think the incentive will work in our favor."

"Well then, why isn't he here?"

"I rather encouraged him to seek some counseling. That may be where he is now."

"Well, I'd like to see this straightened out."

Roslyn spoke up, "I'd like to see that window fixed."

CHAPTER 23

Tuesday, March 22

Ron Looney plunked his frame into the booth and smiled across the table at his partner, Gene Novalchek. Gene was taller than Looney, at six feet, he was at least two inches taller, meaning that Ron had to look up at him even seated. When Ron had once commented to his wife, Meg, that he didn't like looking 'up' at Gene her comment was pithy. "Well, he's really good looking and you shouldn't complain however you get to look at him."

Gene was, in fact, a very pleasant-looking man, favoring his Swedish mother rather than his Polish father, he had a narrow face with prominent eyebrows and intensely dark eyes. His shoulders were always covered in a tailored suit that hid the fact that Gene was a former championship cruiserweight boxer. He was proud that his face did not reveal that background fact, either. Gene was usually smiling, as he was when Ron slid into the booth.

"Hey, partner. Did you order for me?" Looney asked.

"Dude, do I have to do all the work here? I picked the place."

"You always pick this place because Sandy's here. Besides I drove and parked and all that."

"Well, I haven't had a chance to order yet. I'm waiting for her to have time."

"She's the waitress, buddy. She'll make time. Especially for you. How long you two been dating now?"

"A few months."

"Are we ever going to go someplace else for lunch?"

"You can if you want. I'll stick with Sandy and the 'usual' right here."

"I must say, the 'usual' is certainly good, but I'm thinking about getting a cheeseburger." In the many months, the two detectives had taken their lunch where Sandy was waitressing their usual was a patty melt with potato chips and iced tea. Gene stared at Ron like he had grown an extra nose.

"What for?"

"I want a cheeseburger."

"We come for the patty melt."

"No, we come so you can see Sandy. Then you get a patty melt. I, on the other hand, have had enough pattie melts. Or is it patties melt? Anyway, I think I'd like a cheeseburger."

"This is just not right."

Before Ron could make another rejoinder, Sandy was at their table. She had eyes only for Gene, as always. "Want your usual, honey?"

"Yes. Yes, I do," he said staring at Looney.

Sandy turned to Ron and paused a second before asking, "And for you, Ron?"

Somewhat taken aback that Sandy knew his name, Ron hesitated only a second before saying, "Cheeseburger, please, medium rare, with sweet potato fries."

"Iced tea?"

"Yes, please."

Sandy turned and walked away. As always, Ron and Gene watched her walk away before resuming their discussion.

Ron asked, "What's the deal with her knowing my name all of a sudden?"

"What do you mean?"

"We've been coming here for months, months before you starting dating. She's never been the slightest bit interested in me, or my order or anything. Now it's 'and what for you, Ron?' What's going on?"

"Nothing. I just happened to mention your name, that's all."

"Why?"

"Oh, we were talking about how much we love the patty melt here, That's all."

"So, now I'm the bad guy that doesn't want the patty melt?"

"I'm sure she'll get over it," Gene smiled as Sandy brought them their drinks. They watched her walk away again.

"How long did you wait before asking her out?"

"I don't know, a month maybe."

"A month, my foot. Closer to four months, I think. But I'm glad you did. And I want you to treat her really nice."

"I do. And what's your interest anyway."

"We get better service here than anywhere else."

"You are not serious."

"Serious as the Reds bullpen troubles are."

"Wait. That's really serious."

"That's what I'm saying."

The discussion rambled on from there, ranging over the Reds possibilities in the upcoming season, some potential name changes for the Cleveland baseball team, including 'Cleveland Baseball Team' and 'Cleveland Baseball Browns'. Their mood was light because they had just finished a homicide case and given the Assistant District Attorney a basket load of evidence, including a confession.

As was their custom, Ron left his money on the table and went to get the car while Gene stayed and talked a few more minutes with Sandy. They never had coffee at the café and went to the little coffee shop down the block from headquarters when they got back to the office.

They walked back to the office with their coffee and chose the back stairs. The Homicide Division was on the fourth floor of the headquarters building. The division space occupied the southwest corner of the block-sized building. Head-high dividers cordoned off the area with an opening into the center of the floor plan. The area was affectionately known as the "Dick Pen" and was filled with detectives' desks pushed against one another in pairs for partners. The back stairwell entered the floor near the outside corner adjacent to the office of the Captain of the division, Arne Thorason.

The Captain, or 'Thor', was a veteran of the Cincinnati police department and highly regarded within the upper ranks. Much of that regard came from his success as a leader. Some regard, however, likely accrued to him because of his appearance. Thor was a former college middle linebacker, almost six feet tall with broad shoulders and little waistline bulge; he looked ready to plug a hole in the defensive line at any moment.

His bulky body, squarish head, and bushy eyebrows caught immediate attention but what impressed the most were his eyes. Dark and penetrating alone, his gaze could be unnerving. But, when coupled with a tucked head, tight jaw, and glaring from under those brows, "The Look" was feared by everyone, including, it was rumored, the Chief.

Captain Thorason was known to evoke The Look whenever someone failed to meet his standards in the division. For obvious reasons, those occasions were few and far between.

Looney peeked out of the stairwell. Noting that the Captain's door was open, as it usually was, he and Gene used the outer walkway to get to their desks. Ron sat down and pulled out the folder with the final piece of paperwork for the ADA. He signed it and handed it across to Gene for his signature. "I suppose one of us could take the rest of the day and walk that over to the DA's office," he drawled.

Unexpectedly Arne Thorason appeared at Looney's desk. Another of his characteristics was minimal conversation and the multi-faceted use of 'Huh'. Detectives throughout the division argued whether the word was a question, an expression of surprise, a dismissal, or an equivalent of 'I'm still listening'. He looked at Looney for a moment, then asked, "You still friends with that guy at New City?"

"Uh, yes, sir. I am. Why?"

"They got a DB over there. Why don't you guys take it since you're done with that one?" Ron and Gene both recognized that Thor was not asking a question and didn't expect an answer. Each of them got up, grabbed their coat, and headed for the door still holding their fresh cup of coffee.

Going back down the stairs, Gene said, there's one good thing about getting a case at New City."

Ron didn't pause as he asked, "What's that?"

"After all those trips we made over there earlier, we now have a 'usual' at the Green Bean coffee counter."

Ron shook his head, "Gene, my man, you have a fresh cup in your hand."

"Yeah, but that'll be gone by the time we get to New City."

Chapter 24

Tuesday, March 22

The scene at New City was anything but usual. They were directed by the uniformed police officers outside the front entrance to proceed around the building to the office of the Director of Research. Inside that office, they found several people clustered in the outer office. As the detectives entered, however, everyone stepped back and created a path for them to enter the office of the Director where they were presented a gruesome tableau.

Alston MacFarlane was sitting in his chair behind his desk with his throat slit open and most of his blood volume spewed over the general area. His head was thrown back and to the right exposing the slash mark from just below the ear on the left to beyond the midline on the right and passing slightly below the jawline.

After a brief look at the body, the detectives noted the others in the room. Unsurprisingly, there was Kathryn Darringer, the County Medical Examiner. Ron nodded to her and the short woman standing beside her.

"You too, doc?" he said, addressing the shorter woman.

Monique Song, pathologist at New City, nodded her agreement.

Darringer commented, "Seemed right to me to ask Monique to take a look. You know she was the Medical Examiner for Cuyahoga County for five years."

Ron and Gene nodded; they already knew this from another encounter with the diminutive Dr. Song.

"Alright if we walk around?" Ron asked the two pathologists.

They both nodded and he and Gene did their routine of walking the circumference of the scene in opposite directions. At a couple of points, each stopped and looked around them in the room or stooped to look under the desk. Both spent little time looking at the wound itself and more looking at the splay of blood behind the desk, to the side, and over the top.

After their several minutes of perusal, Ron turned to Darringer and asked, "Time? Can't be recent, the blood is all congealed."

Darringer nodded, "We think it was probably late yesterday afternoon or evening. Rigor is starting to resolve."

"Who found him?"

"His secretary. She's in the outer office."

"Last seen?"

"Apparently also the secretary. He was working at his desk when she left yesterday around five o'clock."

Ron walked to the front of the desk and stretched his arm toward the body. Darringer and Song looked at each other and smiled. Gene watched Looney's activity and said, "What're you thinking, partner? Had to be plastic man, right? No normal guy can reach that far."

"Yeah, I'm thinking something like that, all right." He walked back to the left end of the desk and checked the position of the body's feet. He stood up and smiled at the Medical Examiners. "Little puzzle, there, isn't it?"

"Whatever do you mean, detective?" asked Darringer, smiling and looking sideways at Dr. Song.

"I mean I don't think he was sitting at his desk when he was cut. I think he was standing here," he indicated the area behind the desk and close to the left end. "I also think whoever did this was known to him because he got that close. And I think the killer has a familiarity with sharp blades."

Monique spoke up, "That's a lot of thinking, Detective Looney. May I ask for your reasoning?"

"Sure, Dr. Song. First, I don't think anybody could kill this way leaning across the desk. It's too easy for the victim to move away. Second, look at the blood spray behind the desk. That doesn't come from a body in this position," he pointed at the man in the chair facing forward. "So, I think he was standing facing this way," indicating away from the desk behind the left end, "and close enough for the killer to make a clean swipe.

"I think he knew the killer, I think the killer is right-handed and familiar with sharp instruments because this is a single swipe. Wouldn't be surprised if it's a surgical blade, being as it's in the hospital and all."

"Anything else?" asked Darringer.

"Oh, yeah," Looney said smiling at her. "The killer is about the same height as the dead man. The swipe was mostly downward."

"Very good, detective," said Monique. "We came to the same conclusions."

"Well, I'm not surprised," Looney said with a big grin. "You are both pretty smart cookies."

"May I have the body now?" asked Darringer.

"Fine by me," Looney said looking at Gene who also nodded. "Why are you here, doc?" he asked Monique.

Darringer answered, "First, it's her house. Second, she's an old friend and a valued colleague."

"Fair enough. And, completely fine with us," Looney said.

"She also says she has some experience working with you," Darringer said. "And that it wasn't a bad thing."

"Well, I appreciate that, doc. The feeling is mutual." He nodded at Dr. Song. "Now, we'd like to talk to that secretary."

Ron found the secretary in the outer office sitting on a small divan next to Tom Bolling. She was very distraught, and Tom asked that they be quick about questions. The young lady appeared to be bright and capable but was struggling with her emotions. She gave them lucid responses despite her anxiety, but with a shaky voice. MacFarlane often worked past her quitting time, she said. He didn't keep an appointment book; she did not know of anyone scheduled to come to see him the day before. She had no idea who would do such a thing. The only turmoil in the office recently had to do with the cessation of funding to one researcher, Adam Schlecter. She did not know where Dr. Schlecter was. She did say that MacFarlane said Schlecter did not accept the announcement in a gentlemanly fashion. According to the secretary, MacFarlane reported that Schlecter had thrown his coffee cup on the lobby floor and stormed out of the hospital. They took down all her particulars and let her go.

Tom saw that she was properly escorted and then turned to Ron. "We don't know where that guy is either."

"What?"

Tom told the intricate story of Adam's life falling apart, his son's disappearance, his surgical privileges suspended, his wife's death, and, finally, his loss of research funds. The picture was quite convincing. Adam Schlecter was a man with nothing to lose. The detectives thanked Tom and returned to the parking lot.

Sitting in Ron's car, Gene said, "We got nothing else. Let's talk to this surgeon."

"Nobody knows where he is."

"Nobody said they had gone to his house."

Chapter 25

Tuesday, March 22

Captain Thorason indicated he wanted a quick briefing on the murder at New City before the end of the day. Looney gathered the photos and notes from the scene while Gene collected photographs and notes from their visit to Adam Schlecter's house. They made a quick run down the block to get a fresh cup of coffee before going to the Captain's office.

"Think we ought to get him a cup?" Gene asked as they stood in the short line at the coffee counter.

"Why not? Nice gesture and we know how he takes it, Ron answered as he stepped up to make the order.

"Does anyone ever drink the coffee made in the break room?"

"Sometimes. Mostly late at night when the coffee shop is closed, though."

"We oughta think about getting one of those capsule coffee makers. Every cup is fresh, you know? And the guys can buy their own capsules, so everyone isn't drinking the same stuff."

"Good idea, Gene," Ron said, taking the two cups he had purchased as he moved out of the way. "You try to convince everyone to pitch in fifteen or twenty dollars for buying the machine. See how far you get with that."

As they walked back to the police building moments later, Gene said, "You know it would be less expensive in the long run to have one of those machines."

"Try explaining that to the rest of the division. I mean, I'll back you, and I'll be the first to throw in twenty bucks. But I'm not about to take on the task of trying to explain coffee economics to a bunch of cops. Especially when your idea does not come with doughnuts."

They walked up the back stairs and went to the Captain's office first, to set their cups on his desk. Thor looked up at the third cup and nodded to Looney, then went back to sorting through the papers on his desk.

Gene and Ron went to their desks to retrieve their exhibits; on the way back to the Captain's office, Gene said, "Let's try to make this brief, OK? I have a date tonight."

"You have a date every night. Why don't you just marry the girl, and then you can go home to her every night like I do."

"Let's not get into that now. Just remember, it's Date Night."

They sat in front of Thor's desk and waited for him to reach a stopping point in his paperwork. When he did so, and looked up at them, his indication for them to start talking was to pick up his cup and close the file he was working on. Thorason was not a voluble man, often indicating who he expected to speak by looking at them and indicating them to pick up their speed by hand signals. He looked at Looney and nodded.

"Well, Chief, we've got one big mess at New City," he began. With an occasional prompt or further information from Gene, Ron laid out the circumstances: a prominent member of the hospital hierarchy was known to be working late in his office the previous day. His secretary found him murdered at his desk this morning. Time of death was probably late afternoon to the early evening last night. The method of death was a single stroke with a surgically sharp blade across the throat from under the left ear. Forensics indicate the dead man was standing at the end of his desk facing the killer, who we think is right-handed, when he was struck. The killer probably pushed him into his chair and turned it toward the front of the desk. No fingerprints were found on the chair so the killer either wiped the surface or was wearing gloves.

Discussion with the secretary and the chief of staff, who is Ron's old friend, indicated that the dead man had only one possible involvement in a circumstance that might lead to anger or a revenge killing. Ron explained that the dead man had told one of the New City researchers that his funding had been stopped. The decision to stop the funding was not that of the dead man, according to Tom Bolling, but a national funding agency. Further, the researcher had known for months that this was a possibility. However, the two detectives went on to say that their questioning of the dead man's wife gave no other clues to a possible motive. She had not apparently known of the reaction of the researcher to the news of funding cutoff.

Gene explained that Tom Bolling had told them that the researcher had not been seen at the hospital since that time. He had said that the hospital personnel gave the researcher time to accommodate and fully expected him to return to work soon. But he had not and calls to his home and cell phone went unanswered. That's why the two detectives decided to visit the house themselves. Gene slid past the method by which they gained access to the house; at least they hadn't broken the front door. He mentioned that there was ample evidence that the man had left the premises. The closet in the main bedroom was largely devoid of men's clothes; they found clothes hangers on the bed and the floor. There were no toiletries in the bathroom, and two drawers in the highboy were empty and only partially closed. The front hall contained a complete set of flowery luggage and one large brown suitcase with space beside it for two others of smaller size.

The detectives concluded that the researcher had packed his clothes and left the area. They contacted DMV about his vehicle and had put out a BOLO before they came back to the office.

"Huh," said Thorason.

"Yeah," said Ron. He fancied himself a good interpreter of Thor's common monosyllabic comment. He went on, "We can't be sure when he left the house, so we intend to do some more interviewing of the neighbors. Plus, Gene had the idea of checking with the power company to see if there was any sharp jump in usage in the last week since that might be when he was going around the house to clean things out."

Thor nodded and sipped his coffee. Then he raised his eyebrows and looked at each of the detectives briefly.

"That's it, sir. We'll let you know when, and if, we get any more information," Ron said, standing up. Gene stood up as well and Thor, nodded to them as they left the office.

"That was painless," Gene said.

They put their evidence packets away in their desks. Ron looked at him and said, "Usually is, if you're organized and ready for questions."

"He didn't ask any questions," Gene noted.

"Didn't have to. We answered them all," Ron replied and headed for the door.

Chapter 26

Wednesday, March 23

Gene looked at the coffee pot in the break room and put his cup back. He went to his desk and told his partner, "Even when the pot isn't close to empty, it just doesn't look like something you'd drink voluntarily. I mean it's got a greenish-purple sheen over the top."

Looney didn't look up. "We'll get travel cups from the coffee shop."

"Great idea, partner. Now I see why you're the lead."

"Nope. It's because I'm smarter and better looking."

"Well, that's not what Sandy told me."

"Girl needs glasses. Do you ever notice how close she gets to you whenever we go in there? Get your gear. We got a day of interviews and I do need that coffee."

Heading toward the backstairs they passed the open door to the Captain's office. Knowing they weren't coming back right away, Ron decided not to engage Thor about a cup for himself. As they passed the door he looked in quickly and found Thor engaging a folder on his desk with The Look and they hustled past. In the stairwell, Gene asked, "How long has Thor been off the street?"

"Probably close to fifteen years now. He was relatively new when he hired me."

"I heard he was really good on the street. I wonder if he wants to go back. I mean he is taking a lot of interest in this case at New City."

"He doesn't want to go back out. He wants to know we are on top of things because this will be a prominent case around town. Did you notice the story is above the fold in the morning paper?"

"You sure he's not wanting to manage us a little?"

"Did he sound like he was managing?"

"Ah, no. He barely sounded awake."

"That's his deal; you know this. He will let us run our investigation and he will back us all the way up the chain. But if he thinks we are slacking off or chasing rabbits we will have to go to the office and we'll get The Look."

They stood in line for their coffee and Gene decided he would also have a morning bun.

"You better have that eaten before we get to the car. I don't want any crumbs on my floor," Ron warned. That started the argument about whose car should be used all over again. The discussion lasted until they arrived at the hospital.

Gene said, getting off the topic of his dislike for Ron's car, "Before we leave, let's go by the lobby and let Nick make us a 'usual'."

"Ever since he told you that he had a 'usual' for you, you've acted like that's a really big deal."

"He's got a 'usual' for you, too"

"Well then, that's an entirely different story. We will, of course, need to go see Nick while we are here."

But they started in the Research wing. MacFarlane's secretary had returned to work and was sitting at her desk. She looked up and gave them a wan smile. "Good morning, detectives."

"Good morning," Ron said. "Do you have some time to talk further with us?"

"Sure," she said. "Nothing is going on that can't wait. And I can't really think about anything else right now, anyway."

Gene closed the door to the hall and he and Ron took seats in front of her desk.

Ron started by asking, "Would you please tell us your name? We were not really introduced yesterday. I just got that your name is 'Janie'."

"Coombs. Janie Coombs."

"How long had you worked here, Janie?"

"Almost four years. This is my first job. Dr. Mac hired me because I was a biology major in college. He thought I would understand the language better than someone without that background."

"What kind of a man was he?"

"Dr. Mac was rather like my grandfather. He was not much of a conversationalist but he was witty."

"Did he or his job make a lot of enemies?"

"What? No. At least I don't know of any. There were tense times every few months when we did financial sweeps but nobody ever cursed at him or threatened him that I know of."

"What's a financial sweep?"

"It's something to adjust the money and I don't know much about it but Deborah can explain it better."

"Who is Deborah?"

"That's Dr. Mac's Executive Assistant. Her office is right next door."

"Before we talk with her, are you aware of anyone that might have wanted to hurt Dr. MacFarlane?"

"Really no. I mean he did say that Dr. Schlecter was 'raging mad' at him about losing his funding but that wasn't anything Dr. Mac could control."

"All right, could you introduce us to Deborah?"

Deborah Allen turned out to be a fiftyish woman of average height and greater than average girth. Her hair was obviously dyed and she wore too much makeup. She did not stand when the detectives came into her small office and she looked at them over her horn-rimmed glasses with some degree of annoyance.

"Yes?" she said.

"I'm Detective Ron Looney and this is my partner, Gene Novalchek. We are here to follow up on the murder of your boss, Dr. MacFarlane."

"Yes. Bad thing. I wasn't here. I don't know anything."

"Well, you might know if there was someone upset enough with Dr. MacFarlane to want to kill him. Do you?"

"What? Dr. Mac? Of course not. He was a teddy bear. Good at his job and all that but a teddy bear."

"Anyone particularly upset by recent financial sweeps?"

"Huh. Where'd you hear about that?"

"Tell me about those sweeps," Ron said avoiding her question intentionally.

"We do those sweeps every quarter. We look at every researcher's finances and their planned expenditures for the quarter. Almost every time, someone is short and others are long. It's a financial practice to sweep up all the unobligated money a couple of weeks prior to the end of the quarter so we can help anyone who needs a little 'carry-over'."

"Is that legal," Gene pondered out loud.

"Well, if it ain't every research organization in the country should be in jail."

"Has anyone complained about the 'sweep' or been particularly angry at MacFarlane because of it?"

"Everybody who has money taken away is upset but the money isn't lost. They get it back the next quarter. We're only seeing that the whole research program maintains funding equitably. It's certainly not a reason to kill someone."

As they were leaving Deborah's office, Ron wanted to step back into Janie's office to give her a card. He found her talking with a tall, thin young woman in scrubs.

"Oh, detective," Janie said, "This is Allison Meterchson. She's one of the research assistants here. You should ask her about Dr. Schlecter."

"Really? Allison, did you know Dr. Schlecter?"

"I know who he is. That's all, really. But what Janie is hinting at is that I saw him and Dr. Mac in the lobby that day?"

"What day was that?"

"I guess it was the fifteenth. I was getting coffee from the Green Bean and I saw Dr. Schlecter and Dr. Mac. Dr. Schlecter hollered something at Dr. Mac and threw a cup of coffee on the floor and stormed out of the hospital."

"Ah," Ron nodded. "Can you remember what he said?"

"Oh yeah. He said, real loud and all, 'All you SOBs are the same. You all are cutting my throat.' And then he left."

"'Cutting my throat'? Are those his exact words?"

"Oh yes. We all heard him. And he was really mad."

CHAPTER 27

Wednesday, March 23

Ron and Gene decided to go to Schlecter's lab to interview Schlecter's technicians. They found the area without difficulty, but the laboratory initially seemed empty. They went in and started walking around. In the rear of the area, they came across a young man sitting on the floor, looking under cabinets.

"Hello," he said, not getting up.

"Hello, yourself," Gene said. "Whatcha doing?"

"Inventorying glassware. We are going to take over this space next week, and we need to know what's here and what we may need to purchase."

"So, you don't work for Dr. Schlecter?"

"Oh, no. He left, you know. He's no longer funded, so the lab was assigned to my boss.

"Where are the people who worked here for Schlecter?"

"You mean Bonnie and Terry?" I really don't know. Haven't seen them around since Schlecter left, I don't think."

"Who around here would know how to find them?"

"If Janie doesn't know. I'd guess HR."

"Why HR?"

"Because they keep records on all of us; if there's a check coming they'd have the forwarding address."

"Good information. Thanks."

Out in the hall, Ron heard this information and said, "Let's go right to HR. I doubt that Janie has that information."

"Maybe we could go by the lobby to get to HR?" Gene suggested

"Yeah, sure. That's a good idea. I think we may need our 'usuals' before the day is over."

Later, carrying their Green Bean coffee cups, they walked into the HR department and asked for help locating recent employees. The middle-aged man who agreed to help them quickly pulled paper folders on the two laboratory technicians. He indicated the detectives could sit in the entry area seating to review the records, but the records could not leave the area.

Ron looked at Bonnie's record while Gen went through Terry's. Bonnie Phillips was 39 years old and a native of Cuyahoga Falls. She had a degree in laboratory science from Kent State and had worked previously at the Cleveland Clinic before being recruited to join Schlecter's staff. The folder had a local address, and Ron made a note of this. He mentioned that to the Personnelist and was informed that Bonnie had asked that a letter of reference be sent to a laboratory at UCLA. He did not have a forwarding address for her final check.

Ron went back into the entry area and found Gene making notes from Terry's record. The whole record was pretty thin. He was from Las Vegas; had a BS degree from UNLV but no work record or references. Address listing showed an apartment in Las Vegas, another in Akron, Ohio, and one in Cincinnati. Gene had these annotated in his notes.

Meeting again in the hall outside of HR, Ron notes, "You may have noticed, but it's lunchtime, and I'm pretty certain we can get to Sandy's place without missing a beat."

Gene stared at his partner. "What is up with you? First, recognizing that it is the time of day when civilized people partake of food. That's not like you. I mean, you usually want to work right through lunch. But second, choosing the place where I always want to go? You setting me up for something, partner?"

"Yes. I am. I'm thinking we are done at the hospital and will need a lot of telephone work from here on. And you are just the man for that, right?"

"I'm certainly willing to flip you for it. Right after lunch, OK?"

Lunch was somewhat relaxed. They were, as was increasingly the case, back at Sandy's place of work and sitting in a front booth. Sandy had smiled at them from the back when they came in, so they grabbed a couple of menus from the cashier's stand and sat down.

Ron opened his menu and asked, "Why, exactly, do we get menus when we come here? We always get the same thing. Our 'usual'."

"There was that one time you ordered the cheese sandwich."

"That was very early."

"And then yesterday you got a cheeseburger."

"I may do that again. It was a very fine cheeseburger,"

"Well, whatever. Do what you like. I'm sticking with the usual," Gene dismissed the idea of change in his routine.

"You know, Sandy can probably handle a different order now and then. I mean, that's part of her job, isn't it?"

"That's not the issue . . .Hello." His thought shifted as Sandy arrived at their table. She brought two glasses of iced tea and put them in front of the detectives.

"The usual?" She asked, looking at Gene with a big smile.

"Absolutely," he smiled back.

Sandy looked at Ron. "Are you going with the cheeseburger again?"

"Yes, please. It was very good." They smiled at each other briefly.

"Got it. Be right back." She turned and walked back toward the kitchen. Again, as usual, both men watched her walk all the way back.

"Now that's out of the way," Ron said, "how about we think over our 'knowns'?"

Gene toasted the idea with his tea and started the discussion. "Seems like we have a lot of 'knowns' without knowing whether they mean anything."

"Such as?"

"One, the dead guy is well-liked by everybody but had one blow-up over finances in the last month."

"Two," Ron added, "that blow-up was with a missing surgeon."

"Three, the killing was done with surgical skill."

"I'm not certain about that," Ron said, holding up his hand. "I'll take that the weapon probably was a surgical blade, but I'm not sure about the skill thing."

"I would argue 'skill' because of the broad stroke and no hesitation," Gene posited raising his glass.

"Still disagree. You remember we've dealt with Special Operators in the past. They train to perform that exact move. Quick stroke, no hesitation. Cut the larynx to prevent the victim from crying out."

Gene put his glass down and thought a moment before nodding slowly, "OK. Point made. I'll back my 'known' down to 'killing was done with surgical-like skill'. How's that?"

"Can't disagree. Got a Number Four?"

"Only if I unpack number Two and mention all those things we know about the missing surgeon."

"Who could be away on a trip."

"Or who could be escaping the scene of the crime."

"Or that," Ron noted as he moved his glass of tea to allow Sandy to put in front of him the platter with his cheeseburger and fries.

She put the plate with Gene's 'usual' patty melt and chips in front of him and adjusted it several times while she smiled at him. Ron grabbed the pepper shaker as Sandy left and noted, "That's not a lot of 'knowns' to work on, partner."

"Yeah, I know. But we're just getting started. The phone calls are gonna pay off, I bet."

Later, while Ron was bringing the car to the front of the café so Gene could spend a little time talking with Sandy, he began to devise a plan for those telephone calls and which one to assign to Gene.

Even later, as they compared their notes, they had to agree they didn't have much to add to the list of 'knowns'. Ron's call to the laboratory at UCLA successfully reached Bonnie Phillips. She was completely unaware of the recent events at New City and was appalled at the murder of "Dr. Mac". She referred to him as 'a sweet old guy' and said she was sure he would not have engaged anyone in a violent argument. She described Schlecter as a moody fellow who was very bright but more of an 'absent researcher' in the lab until recently. She described her knowledge of him over four years and told Ron what her lab role was. When asked about Terry, she admitted she didn't know much about him; he was from Las Vegas and was in Ohio attempting to get into one of the state's medical schools. She said she had not seen either Schlecter or Terry after each had left the laboratory that morning.

Gene's call to the Las Vegas address allowed him to talk with Terry's mother. She seemed distracted and had to be reminded during the call what she had been asked. She apparently did know that Terry was in

Cincinnati, but she did not have an address or a telephone number for him. He apparently called her every two or three weeks and told her his plans for medical school. She had not heard from him in almost three weeks. She promised to have him call Gene if he contacted her. Gene was very uncertain about that promise.

"New 'knowns'?" Ron asked, leaning back in his chair.

"The surgeon is potentially violent."

"Not a big 'known' to me."

"Or me. I'm going home. We can look around town for the guy tomorrow."

CHAPTER 28

Thursday, March 24

S am Mastone did not have much interest in the discussion items at the morning meeting. When Roslyn pushed on the subject of employee education as a major interest and movement of interest to the Head Office, Sam simply nodded. Even when Tom and Roslyn got into a discussion about the style of the effort and whether it required new nursing personnel to direct the effort, Mastone was distant and dismissive.

He showed slightly more interest in a progress report from the head of the committee on the development of a child care center on the grounds of the hospital. The idea of the center had generated a good deal of discussion in the past. There were questions about its location, the capacity it might have, operating hours, qualifications of parents of the children accepted into the center, what ages would be accepted, should there be accommodation for 'part-time' users, etc. For every one of these options, Sam Mastone had an opinion and an argument to back it up. And, for every point in the discussion, Sam was usually the first to speak. Now, however, he seemed to only be passingly interested in the topics and only if there was a financial step he needed to approve.

Beverly brought up the need for a complete revision of the telephone trees used by the divisions for emergency notifications.

Such an item would typically be micro-managed by Mastone, but his interest was clearly not in the discussion. Tom suggested he would write a memorandum for the director to sign and circulate directing each division to update their tree and their website information about emergencies. Sam nodded and indicated he felt that would satisfy the need.

Roslyn asked if Tom knew whether Adam Schlecter had been arrested yet.

He looked at her steadily for a moment and then said, "I am not aware that he has been found. And I do not know why he would be arrested."

She looked down her nose, "Surely you understand that it must have been him who killed Dr. MacFarlane."

"I don't know any such thing."

"Then where is he, and why isn't he explaining his innocence."

"Again, I don't know where he is. I do know that people are innocent until proven guilty, however."

"What about your policeman friend? Doesn't he think Adam did it?"

"Roslyn, I don't know what Detective Looney thinks. I do know that we all wonder where Adam is."

"Well, I always thought he was a little too intense," Roslyn said looking at the ceiling light fixtures. Beside her, Alena Preston nodded in agreement.

Mastone indicated the meeting had gone on long enough and as people were rising to leave, he indicated for Tom and Beverly to remain.

"Listen, Tom," he said when the room had cleared, "I don't want to be the face of this murder here at New City. You need to talk to the press and handle things like you did that last time."

Tom felt a small degree of warmth and appreciation from the director with that comment. He noted, "I don't think we're going to have to have much presence in the story. But, if you like, I can contact the paper and tell them to come to me for any comment."

Whereas Sam Mastone usually felt there was no such thing as bad publicity, he did not want personal linking between him and the murder of a prominent scientist. "That would be fine, Tom. Tell them we are very concerned and looking forward to the police catching the perpetrator."

Tom nodded, thinking to himself, 'He can't even call the guilty guy a murderer. He's a perpetrator.' To the director, he said, "I'll take care of it, Sam." Then, nodding to get Beverly moving with him, they left the conference room.

On the way back to their offices, Tom said, "I am not going to be sticking my neck out in the press. I'd like for you and Taliaferro to contact Edderman and tell him there may be some off-record comment from me at some time but not right now."

Tom referred to Johnny Taliaferro, the Public Affairs Officer for New City. That would be appropriate for him to contact Dan Edderman, a daily columnist in the local paper. A few years back, Edderman uncovered a connection between the death of a local high school basketball player and a local drug ring. Since then, Edderman's column, Daniel's Den, was a highlight in the paper, and Dan himself an investigative journalist. Tom and Looney had dealt with him successfully before concerning a serious problem at New City, and they had an arm's length relationship since. Tom wanted to keep the major headlines about the murder and New City on page three or after. Edderman might help with that. Of course, he might also bite the hand.

Chapter 29

Monday, March 28 AM

Looney got the call as he stepped out of the shower. Another body was found on the facility grounds at New City. He called to Meg and asked for a cup of coffee to go and then hurriedly dressed. As he came down the stairs Meg met him at the door with both the requested cup and a breakfast burrito she had quickly prepared.

"Whatever did I do before I found you?" he asked slipping into his coat and grabbing a quick kiss before heading out the door armed with his traveling breakfast.

"I think you went without eating a lot of the time," she said to his disappearing back.

Novalchek got the call at about the same time but he was still lying in bed. He jumped up and grabbed his clothes, dressing quickly but taking care to ensure that the shirt was properly tucked and the tie correctly tied. He left his house without either breakfast or coffee.

They arrived within a minute of each other at the provided address, the fourth floor of the New City hospital parking deck. A uniformed officer at the entrance had opened the gate for them and told them who was already on the scene. They parked next to each other and nodded in the direction of the other as they walked the last few yards to an area roped off with crime scene tape. Another uniformed officer nodded to them and raised the tape for them to enter the area.

"Morning, Doc," Looney said as he approached the Medical Examiner standing near the body of a man in a suit lying in an empty parking space between two cars. Darringer looked at him from under her eyebrows and said, "Detective."

"What do we have, then?" Ron asked

"Forty-eight-year-old man. Probably killed late last night by a slashing cut to the carotid."

Ron looked quickly at the body and back at Darringer, "Like the other one?"

"See what you think?" she replied without looking up from her documentation.

Ron and Gene stepped over to the body which was partially draped with a sheet. At their signal, one of Darringer's assistants pulled the sheet back and the detectives did their individual 360-degree circle around the body in opposite directions. Ron stooped down to look closely at the neck wound and remained there until Gene joined him.

"Looks like a repeat," Gene said. Ron nodded and they both stood. Ron became aware of Tom Bolling standing just inside the restraining tape, wearing a dark overcoat. He went over and asked, "This one of yours?"

"Yes," Tom said soberly. "It's Harry Finkbeiner, one of our anesthesiologists."

"Connection to Dr. Mac?"

"Other than they were both on the staff here, I don't know."

"How'd you hear?"

"Security called me at home early and I came right away. Your people were all over the place, securing the scene and making the staff park someplace else."

Ron heard the annoyance in Tom's voice and quickly said, "We'll get out of your hair as soon as we can, Tom. I promise." He went back to talk to Darringer.

"Doc, Gene and I think it's pretty similar. You got anything else for us here?"

"From what Monique and I put together, he was opening his car door and someone came up behind him and got him to turn around. There may have been a conversation; we can't be sure. The car door was unlocked and this guy had put his briefcase in the passenger seat. But he was standing beside the car and facing the rear when he was slashed. And Monique and I both agree this is exactly like the other one."

"Dr. Song already been here and gone?"

"Oh, yes. I called her when I got the call. She got here first and made sure the building was secured."

"You checked the site?"

"Completely. Both of us. I didn't see anything other than the body. I expect you'll do your own search."

"You bet. But we're gonna move fast so's we don't disrupt the hospital too much."

"Uh-huh. Whatever," she said losing interest in the discussion and indicating that the assistants could now load the body in the van for removal back to the morgue.

"You'll call if there's something we need to see, right doc?"

"Of course, detective. Of course."

Gene was using a strong flashlight to examine the area beneath the two cars bracketing the body. Ron walked back to the edge of the tape and began a slow walk back toward the position of the body closely examining the surface area. Neither of them found anything particular and a few minutes later stood together watching the morgue van leave.

"If this is the same guy, he might have known what this guy's car looked like and staked it out," Ron said. Gene nodded without speaking and they turned their attention to the ground area on the other side of the parking area. A few cars were parked there but they found no evidence of someone lying in wait; no cigarette butts, candy wrappers, or drink cans were evident.

"So, must've followed him up here," Gene allowed.

"Seems possible. But he could have been waiting and just not very long."

"Either way, it involves some planning and intent, right?"

"Definitely, partner. Definitely. No question this is Murder One. And this is looking more and more like we may have a serial on our hands."

Chapter 30

Monday, March 28 PM

They took up the usual seating arrangement in the Captain's office. Arne Thorason was behind the desk, and Ron and Gene sat in front. The Captain looked up from his paperwork and raised his eyebrows at Ron.

"This is starting to look really grisly, Cap'n," he said. Without waiting for any signal, he continued. "This second death looks almost exactly like the first one. Same slash, probably the same or a similar blade. The docs think the positioning was similar, too. Looks like the killer was facing the guy for a discussion or something and struck."

Gene nodded at his partner's presentation and added, "And nothing left on the ground or in the area to help with identification."

The Captain also nodded and said, "Huh."

Looney went on, "But we did get some information from Dr. Bolling. That's my friend at New City. He said there is a connection between the MacFarlane murder and this one."

The Captain's eyebrows rose.

"Tom says this second guy was the anesthesia guy on one of Schlecter's recent cases where the patient died."

"Huh."

"Yeah, right. Schlecter had his surgical privileges removed because of that death. So, maybe there's a connection in that Schlecter may be thinking that these guys somehow let him down. I mean, the research guy, MacFarlane, was at the very least the bearer of bad news, and maybe he thinks this anesthesia guy contributed to the patient dying. Maybe."

Gene followed up, "You remember we went to this Schlecter guy's house. It looked like he split town. But we found some information at the house that suggested he had a club membership downtown. Also, the financial guys ran his records for us. Doesn't look like he spends a lot of time away from home or hospital but he had a gym membership. This club he joined last year has rooms for rent. That seems a little odd for a guy living here in town, right? We're gonna check those out first thing."

The Captain's left eyebrow rose quickly.

Looney jumped into the conversation. "We can actually check those out tonight to be certain he is not holed up there. It's unlikely since the paper has been linking him to our investigation. I kinda think somebody would've ratted him out by now if he had stayed local. But we'll get right on it."

"Huh."

"Last thing, Cap'n," Ron said, "we did finally talk with one of his laboratory assistants. We found this Bonnie Phillips out in California. She says she never saw Schlecter after he learned about his research funding being stopped. Both he and the other assistant just walked out and never came back. And she stuck around for the rest of the day, cleaning up things and getting ready to leave. If one or the other had come back to the lab, she says she would have seen them. She did say that Schlecter was occasionally moody, but she said she never saw him take out anger on a person. He would just break glassware and stuff."

"Huh."

"Bonnie said he was a little 'mercurial'." He looked at Thor and at Gene, and then continued, "I looked it up. It means that a person has mood swings and is unpredictable."

Thor continued to look at Ron.

"We haven't found the other assistant yet. We did find his apartment and talked with his roommate. Got some paperwork about jobs and medical school applications and stuff. Everybody says he's a quiet guy, wanted to go to medical school."

Gene added, "I talked to his mother. She may have been drunk or high on something when we talked. I had trouble getting a straight answer, but she says she doesn't know where he is. She thought he was still here in Cincinnati. She usually hears from him every couple of weeks by telephone but nothing for almost a month now. No cards or letters, so no postmarks."

"Huh."

After a brief silence, the two detectives looked at each other and spoke simultaneously.

"OK, then. We're on our way to that club," said Looney as he rose from his seat.

"Yeah. That's where we're going. Right now," Gene said.

As they got in Ron's car a few minutes later, Gene asked, "So, was that last 'Huh' a question?"

Ron slowly shook his head. "It's all in the context, partner. All the 'huhs' were connected to the eyebrow. They all meant, "hurry up" and get your job done."

Chapter 31

Tuesday, March 29

Ron moved his water glass around in circles on the tabletop. They were back in the café where Sandy worked, their lunch order was being prepared, and their morning had so far been a big zero. Both men were silent until Gene said, "Well, it's not all bad. Now we are pretty sure that he has not been hiding out at the club or the gym."

"Sure," Ron said without inflection, "additional boxes checked in the Negative column could be viewed as progress from somebody's perspective."

"You think Thor has that perspective?"

"He does not now nor has he ever had such a perspective. Thor is completely interested in the positive. That's what he considers us 'doing our job'. These new negatives will not make him happy."

"So, let's not tell him. I mean, let's not tell him right away. Let's wait until we have something positive; then we tell him the things that didn't work out."

"Gene, he probably already knows."

"How could he know. No one was there but us. We didn't tell him."

"If we had something, we would have immediately gone back to keep him apprised, right? Let the boss know we are digging deep and coming up with treasure. That's what we would've done, right?"

"Well, yeah, I guess."

"No guessing. We would have. Maybe even would've called him from the site."

"So . . . Our 'no news' will be seen as 'bad news', is that what you mean?"

"Exactly, and we gotta go get something positive to take back . . ."

Sandy showed up at that moment with their lunch and placed their plates in front of them. She was perceptive enough to notice that neither of them looked at her when they mumbled thanks; she moved off after filling their drink glasses.

After a bite of his patty melt, Gene said, "What's your idea about finding something positive? You gonna meet with J.J. and John?" referring to his partner's routine of having an evening of jazz listening as he tried to make sense of difficult cases. Ron had once explained the habit to him as dating back to his early days in the Air Force. Unmarried and stationed near Kaiserslautern, Germany at the Sembach Air Force Base, Ron had found a small bar that catered to Americans. The local band played jazz and blues and had a considerable following on the base. Ron liked sitting there and sipping a beer and listening. He discovered that very often on the morning after one of those evenings, he suddenly had an insight into the difficult case he was involved with. After paying particular attention to the phenomenon, Looney decided this was the way to help things get 're-arranged' in his head, rather like the unstructured theme in jazz numbers. Initially, the major jazz artists he enjoyed were J.J. Johnson and John Coltrane; Gene latched on to their names and now referred to Ron's problem-solving period as a consultation with "J.J. and John."

Looney looked at this partner wryly and commented, "If it was all that easy, I'd just have the boys on the player when I got home at night, every night. None of our cases would go beyond two days."

"Well, this certainly seems like the time when we could use some outside help."

"Doesn't work that way. We don't have anything to work with. When I spend a night with J.J. and John, it's because we have a jumbled picture and I need to get the various positives lined up correctly. We got no positives here. I got nothing to work with."

There was silence for a few minutes while they made their way through their food. Then Ron looked up and said, "I may not have told you, but a lot of that now depends on Meg."

"How?"

"She somehow senses when the time is right and cooks me a fried chicken dinner with all the Fixin's."

"How'd she get in the picture?"

"I wasn't married in Germany. After we got married, I tried the all-nighter at a local bar once or twice. She didn't care much for that. And the discussion ended up with me explaining the process as a way of solving crimes. She doesn't like me spending the night out at some jazz bar, so now she arranges my favorite meal and gives me the house for the evening. And you know I've got that killer sound system and every jazz record I could want."

"OK, then. We really got to get us some positives."

Ron nodded. "Right now, I feel like we have several pieces to different jigsaw puzzles."

Gene smiled at this analogy and said, "What we really need is the picture on the front of the box, right?"

Ron finished his meal and chased the last bite with half a glass of iced tea. "Want to run the 'knowns'? again?"

"Sure," Gene said and pushed his plate over to the edge so Sandy could pick it up easily. "Any reasons to think our first ones need revision?"

"Nope. I still think we're right about the kills being done with surgical-like expertise, probably using a surgical knife."

"And we have only one suspect who might want to kill these two guys."

"Agreed. And he happens to be a surgeon."

"So, we have that going for us."

"And he has disappeared."

"Except for showing up for a second killing."

"And then disappearing again."

"We haven't found his car. Not at this house. Maybe he's living in it somewhere."

"Did we get that BOLO out on the car yet?"

"I think so, I'll call Ronnie in Dispatch to check."

"Why do you think he went after the anesthesia guy?"

"Tom thinks he was really upset about the patient's death and the lifting of his privileges."

"Why is he blaming the anesthesia guy? Wasn't there another surgeon helping him, or some nurse?"

"I don't know. Probably. Maybe he couldn't find that other surgeon. I don't know."

"Now we're starting a list of Unknowns."

"Or 'don't knows'."

Gene thought for a moment and then asked, "If Tom thinks these murders are connected at the hospital, maybe we should be asking him if anyone else is at risk."

CHAPTER 32

Wednesday, March 30

All the players took their respective seats across the conference table from each other at the morning meeting. Tom tried smiling and nodding a greeting to the nurse executives as they entered, but their response was muted at best. Beverly had warned Tom that Sam Mastone had been asking questions about the cost of dialysis and that he likely had something to discuss that issue.

Tom had his own issue of concern that morning, however. Once Sam entered and went through the usual drill of announcing what everyone already knew about the previous day's activities, Tom spoke up, "Sam, the clinical chairs have once again come to me with a request for access to the workload and financial data we review."

Unabashed, Sam replied, "They get a copy of the report every morning."

"You know that's not what they are talking about. They want access to the data to do their own analysis. They want to drill further down to get at the basic causes."

"We know what's causing them to fall behind, Tom. They need more volume."

"Sam, you know it's not that simple. Volume of what and when? These are smart people, Sam. Give them a chance to come up with their own analyses and improvements."

"How are they going to do any analysis?"

"And you know the answer to that, too. They want the funding for a clinical data analyst that answers their questions."

"Bridge too far, Tom. We've got Andy and his team available to them for analysis. And we have no money for additional analysts."

"Every time they ask Andy for help with something, it conflicts with some project you are doing, and they never get any of his time. We really need to make this happen, Sam."

After a brief silence, Sam took a deep breath and asked, "Why don't you just contract the dialysis activity and take the savings to support such an analyst?"

"What are you bringing that up for? You been talking to one of those dialysis washateria guys?"

"I don't understand that term, but, yes, I have been in consultation with the folks at the downtown center."

Tom took a deep breath and said, "Let me guess. You did some kind of analysis that produced a magic 'cost' for a dialysis treatment, and they gave you a much lower figure to capture our workload."

Sam was only momentarily taken aback that Tom understood what had happened. "What makes you say that?"

"Because they were all over me a year ago with that same argument. They didn't have our actual figures back then, so they were presenting me with their 'guesstimate' and then quoted me a figure for a dialysis procedure that was nearly $50 cheaper."

Sam nodded, regained his composure, and said, "That's a lot of money, Tom, considering all the patients we have and how often they are dialyzed."

"It's all fake, Sam. I sat down with Jim Donaldson and went through the numbers. Those guys downtown are pulling a fast one."

The nurse executives indicated they were disinterested in the discussion and were excused.

Tom went on, "Those guys gave you a 'per dialysis' cost figure, didn't they?"

"Yes, but . . ."

"And you asked Andy to calculate our 'per dialysis' cost for comparison, right?"

"I did, and the difference is almost exactly $50 per treatment, Tom. We need to think hard about why we would not go with contracting out the treatment."

"Did you ask to see the data? Do you know what went into the costing calculations for both numbers?"

A pause before Sam said, "Well, I think they were pretty much the same."

"Not true, Sam. Their cost per treatment is pretty clean; nursing time, dialysate, lines, and medicine for the treatment. That's it. But our cost, because we don't have an accounting system like theirs was done by Andy pulling all costs for any dialysis patient during the year and dividing by the number of dialysis treatments. I know this because Andy came and asked me if he had missed anything. And he had and I told him.

Our costs incorporate 'procedure costs' very similar to the downtown figures plus 'patient costs' including any hospitalization for any patient, and surgical care for their access or anything, all their other medications, and laboratory tests and X-rays."

Sam moved uncomfortably in his chair.

"And that's not all. We support an organ transplant program. For the dialysis population, the support for kidney transplantation, the 'program costs', add additional money into our numerator for things like harvesting, organ preservation, cross-matching, and HLA typing. When you put all those costs into a numerator and divide by the number of dialysis treatments, it's no wonder our figures are higher. And the truth is, Sam, we would continue to bear all those other costs for the patient and the program even if we did contract out the actual treatments."

"I didn't know all that."

"And that's why the clinical chairs should have their own ability to make these calculations and deal with such issues."

"All right. No more talk of contracting. Or extra analysts."

Tom sighed. Putting out fires was an essential part of his job as chief of staff, but it was annoying to know that the fires he had to deal with were the result of arson. Even more so when he knew the arsonist was on the hospital payroll.

Changing the subject, he said, "I talked with the police about the murders, and they are concerned there may be others in the hospital at risk."

"What? Why? Do they know where Schlecter is?"

"No. And remember, we still don't know who is responsible for these murders."

"I never did trust that man."

"What do you mean?"

" I thought he acted kind of dodgy. Wouldn't look me in the eye."

"Really? How often did you engage him in conversation?"

"There was this once in an elevator …"

"Where he shouldn't be talking about patients."

"Whatever. I just thought he was untrustworthy."

"I'm asking Beverly to probe the possibility that there may be some other connection to determine the risk for others. Just wanted you to know."

"I think we need better lighting in the parking areas. I'm going to have Engineering make that happen."

"That sounds appropriate, Sam. Just don't contract out our chemotherapy to pay for it. OK?" He smiled at Sam, who pursed his lips and made a slight nod.

CHAPTER 33

Friday, April 1

Tom was still irritated about his encounter at the morning meeting an hour later as he sat at his desk reviewing reports. He found himself replaying comments and losing track of the information he was reviewing. To break the chain, he got up from his desk and began walking around the room, pacing from the desk to the door and back.

During his third trip to the door, his desk phone rang. Almost no one outside the hospital knew that number. Tom assumed it was medical business and returned to his seat, picked up the phone, and said, "Bolling."

"Hey, doc. I thought it was about time we talked." Tom recognized the scratchy voice on the line.

"Mr. Edderman, how are you?" he said, almost falling into the 'good ole boy' accent he had used with the reporter in times past.

"I'm actually just fine, doc. Thanks for asking. Now that the pleasantries are out of the way, what can you tell me about the killings at New City?"

Tom sat still for a moment, thinking about his previous dealings with Dan Edderman. He and Ron had used him to get a story into print about previous trouble at New City that allowed for some praise to reflect on the hospital. And they had made an unofficial pact to provide Edderman with inside information at times if he would help keep New City out of the headlines. In return, the reporter agreed tnot to publish certain information about police dealings during the investigation to get a full story at the end.

Tom said, "I would imagine you already know as much as I do."

"I know that two doctors at New City have been killed. Their throats were slashed and one of your surgeons is a 'person of interest'. That's what I know. What else is there about this?"

Tom began to slip into the ole country doctor voice. "Well now, There's really not much else about the case that I can say, right now."

"So, there is something. You're just not talking."

"Not what I meant, at all. Detective Looney has not talked to me to any degree about the progress in the case. All I know is just what you said."

"What about this surgeon that's missing?"

"C'mon, Mr. Edderman. He's just missing and they would like to talk to him. I think that's all."

"You don't think a throat-slitting murder and a missing surgeon are connected? C'mon yourself, doc. We had an agreement. You keep me informed and I'll help keep a lid on things about the hospital that are unproven."

"I remember our arrangement. I do not recall that I was to provide you with inside information from the police investigation. Call Detective Looney for that."

"I'm not asking you for police information. I asked about the surgeon. Who is he? What's he done? Why do you think he's running?"

"Whoa, whoa, whoa. Hold on. No one has said he's running."

"Well, why can't he be found if he isn't running?"

Tom thought about that for a moment before answering, "I don't know, but it is entirely possible that he went off the grid for other reasons."

"What are these other reasons, doc? Is he under investigation for other issues?"

Tom bit his lip, realizing that Edderman had tricked him into a revelation he didn't want to be made known. "Look, there was a circumstance here at the hospital shortly before the murders that was very upsetting to Dr. Schlecter, so I suggested he take a sabbatical. It is very likely that he did so and is unaware that the police are interested in talking to him."

"Schlecter, huh? What kind of surgeon is he?"

Tom thought, 'Why did I say his name?' but aloud he said, "General surgeon. And a fine researcher."

"Where did you send him for a sabbatical?"

"I did not send him anywhere. I suggested he might consider doing so. It was always entirely up to him as to when and where. He did not confide in me, and I do not know where he is." Tom's voice was no longer the ole country doctor; it took on the tone and pacing of a one-star general.

Clearly, Dan Edderman picked up on the change. "OK, doc. That's fine. I'll call your buddy Looney about police things. Thanks for the information. Later."

As he hung up the phone, Tom wondered whether Edderman was being polite as he signed off. Tom thought it actually sounded more like a threat.

CHAPTER 34

Tuesday, April 5

Ron sat down in the booth heavily. "That's the third BOLO report on Schlecter's car. And, once again, it was gone when we got there. This is crazy."

Gene nodded. "Yeah, but remember, his car is not all that rare around here. Dark blue 2019 Mercedes E320. Got to be a couple hundred in the county."

"Then why haven't we had a couple of hundred sightings?"

"People are being careful, that's all."

"I'm beginning to think he's not even here anymore."

"Who do you think was responsible for the second slashing, then?"

"I mean, I bet he ran as soon as that was done."

"Why do you think that, partner?"

"Well, one, because we know from the financial guys that he took over three thousand dollars out of his checking account. Two, he packed up clothes and left home. But most of all, three, we can't find him in this city!"

"We can't find him because he's not using his credit cards. Probably one reason he got all that cash. He's not going to any of his old haunts. And I think he's living in his car and moving around a lot. That's why we can't find him."

Both men remained silent until time to order lunch. While waiting for their food, Ron raised the issue of a serial killer again.

Gene's response was, "I would prefer to wait until we had more information."

"Like what? a third murder?"

"Well, not to put such a gruesome note on it, but yes. Three would make me think more 'serial' than just two. Especially since these two have some connection through the hospital and all that."

"I'm afraid we are missing something other than our surgeon friend. I could imagine a hospital-based killer, one with surgical skills like we have supposed, starting his spree in a familiar area. Like the hospital. Then, he begins to expand his horizons and moves outside the hospital into the parking area. Maybe the next victim is not connected to the hospital but is several blocks away."

"You are gonna give me an ulcer, thinking that way. We would have no chance to stop a killer like that. We would be down to just plain luck to have anything to go on."

"I already feel like we're down to just plain luck. And so far, if we didn't have bad luck we wouldn't have any luck at all."

"Speaking of bad luck, the guy I had doing my taxes has retired and I need a recommendation."

"I recommend you do your own taxes."

"I don't have the time. It's too complicated."

"Do you have some stock or land holdings I don't know about, partner?"

"What? No. I just don't understand the questions on those forms. I never did. That's why I always have somebody do the filing for me."

"Well, actually I do, too," Ron said, sipping his tea to conceal his smile.

"Really? Mr. big shot 'do it yourself'? And you got somebody doing yours?"

"For several years, actually."

"Well, tell me. Maybe he can do mine."

"Nope. First, it isn't a 'he'. Second, its Meg."

"Your wife does your taxes?"

"Yep. She's good at it, too. We get a refund almost every year."

"Will she do mine?"

"Nope. But I'll ask her if she knows anyone looking for an easy buck."

"Easy it's not," Gene said. "Thanks."

After eating, Sandy indicated she wanted to talk to Gene, so Looney walked slowly back to his car and waited several minutes before pulling around to the front of the café to pick Gene up. By custom, they went to the small coffee shop down the street from headquarters after parking the car and took their coffee back to the office.

Ron was shuffling through the two murder books on his desk and noting the paucity of information when he realized that Captain Thorason was standing beside him.

"Cap'n."

"Just got a call from a construction crew out west on Baltimore Ave. They got a body. You should check it out."

"Uh, OK. We aren't getting anywhere on this one, anyway."

"Huh."

Gene had overheard the conversation and quickly drained his cup and grabbed his jacket. He met Ron near the door to the stairs. As they started down, he asked, "Why is Thor sending us on this case?"

"Don't know. Don't care. It's something to do and maybe make progress."

They found the construction site with a little difficulty and parked where they could see the crime scene tape. As they approached the area, a man wearing a hardhat saw them and came over.

"Detectives?"

"Right. Looney and Novachek." They showed their badges.

"I'm Jerry Jenkins. Foreman on this job. We were clearing brush off the property where there's some houses to be built. One of my guys was driving a backhoe earlier and heard something that made him look down and realized he had run over a body."

"Where?"

"Right over here," Jenkins said and walked them to the area where small and medium-sized bushes had been uprooted and crushed. The area was littered with tracks from heavy equipment; some of the tracks were filled with standing water from recent rain. Toward the center of the taped off area, Ron could see what appeared to be a torso covered with dirt and brush. He and Gene made their way cautiously to the body, careful not to leave footprints.

Gene put on gloves and cleared some of the brush away from the torso to disclose that the backhoe had driven over the head, crushing the skull and neck. A quick examination revealed that small animals had been at work even before that; fingers were missing and the chest had been invaded by bite marks and infested with insects. The remainder of the corpse was covered with dirt and debris from the clearing project.

"This isn't new," Gene said.

"Nope. The animals have had plenty of time to erase any identity."

Ron turned back to the supervisor. "Have you kept everybody out of this area?"

"Oh yeah. I had some construction tape and put it up around a wide area, and called off work for the day. All the workers are still here if you need to interview anyone."

"Good. Thanks. Right now, I want to look over the site before it gets dark. Ask everyone to sit down somewhere and tell them we'll get to their testimony as soon as we can.

Ron and Gene did their circumspection of the body and nearby area walking in opposite directions. They began at the body and slowly increased the radius of their search area. Nearly twenty minutes passed without much conversation between them until Ron stooped over a picked up something from the ground. A moment later, he called out to Gene, "Hey, partner. You are not gonna believe this."

"Why? Whatcha got?" Gene slowly approached Ron's position.

"I have a wallet. Complete with identification and a credit card."

"OK. That's a break."

"It's more than that. It's a giant leap."

"Why? Who is the guy?"

"The wallet says our dead guy is one Terry Demming."

"Really? Our Terry Demming? From Las Vegas?"

"This is his wallet."

"No wonder he hasn't called his mother in several weeks."

"That's what it looks like."

"How did Thor know?"

"I don't know. He's a mystery. But I bet we know how to find out."

Ron called Jerry Jenkins away from the group of workers and asked, "Are you the one who called the police?"

"Yes. Why?

"Did you talk to a Captain Thorason?"

"I'm not really sure. I was transferred to Homicide. But it was a Captain that I spoke to."

"Uh-huh. And exactly what did you tell him?"

"I said we had found a body out here, that's all.

"No, I'm sure you said more than that. Think. What else did you say?"

'Uh, I think he asked me to describe the body and I told him we had run over the head."

"Keep thinking. What else did you say?"

After a brief thought, Jenkins looked at Ron and said, "I told that Captain that the body was wearing surgical scrubs."

CHAPTER 35

Wednesday, April 6

First, they went to the coffee shop before making their way back to the office. They used the back stairs without speaking and quickly moved past the door to the Captain's office. Back at their desks, Looney deposited the plastic bags containing the relevant items they had collected.

Primary among those was the worn, slim leather wallet containing the driver's license of Terry Demming, Aged 24 of Las Vegas, Nevada. There were two one-dollar bills carefully folded behind the license but no credit cards or other material.

"Pretty meager, I'd say," Gene said.

"Well, we knew he didn't have the proverbial pot. You saw his bedroom in that apartment. No pictures, two changes of clothes, no shoes."

"Yeah. Sad. Taken out so young and never had a chance."

"Does puzzle me a bit, though. His car being so far away."

The local police had covered the area around the construction site where the body was found and had notified Ron and Gene about finding an abandoned car about a quarter-mile away. A quick check on registration and license plate confirmed it belonged to Terry. The detectives had examined the car quickly, looked in the trunk, glove compartment, and under the seats without finding anything striking. They called for the car to be towed away and examined by a forensic team.

"Why?" Gene asked, putting his feet on the desk and leaning back to ponder his partner's puzzlement and explanation.

"Well, we didn't see any gross evidence that he was killed in the car."

"Right."

"So, assuming he was made to drive there, the killer may have left some evidence of his presence in the car."

Gene frowned briefly and asked, " Do you think the killer then walked him a good distance before killing him? Why?"

"Maybe he wanted to use the construction area to hide the body?"

"Then why park so far away? The killer ran some kind of risk that Terry might try to get away. He would have to control him closely."

"Why didn't he take the car when he left?"

"Maybe he had another car closer to the construction."

"You think Schlecter parked near the construction and then walked to find and capture Demming?"

"Well, if Schlecter did this, this would've been the first murder. And he sure would want his own car, I think. Don't you?"

"Well, remember, we haven't a clue about the whereabouts of that car of his. Hard to say if it was gone before this murder or not. But it's surely gone now."

"Still troubles me about Terry's car being so far away from where he was killed."

"You sure that's where he was killed?"

"Well, truthfully, no. But I do not believe anyone would kill him where they parked that car, and then carry him a quarter-mile to hide the body."

"Yeah. I agree. It's a puzzle. But you do think this was Schlecter, right?"

"Well, yeah," Looney leaned forward and put his head in his hands to stare across the desk at Gene. "We need to re-order our 'knowns' a bit. I still think this fits with Schlecter. Maybe something we don't know about the lab work or the fact that the research was canceled. Maybe Schlecter thought that Terry didn't do enough to help him succeed. Another case of someone letting him down at a critical point."

"Yeah, that fits, all right. But there's something that bothers me . . ."

The phone on Ron's desk rang and interrupted Gene's thought. Ron nodded to him and reached for the receiver.

"Homicide. Walker."

"Hello, detective." The raspy voice was all too familiar to Ron, and he responded quickly, "What do you want, Edderman?"

"What I always want, detective. Inside scoop. Things others don't know. That's all."

"Why are you calling me?"

"Because your buddy, Bolling wasn't very forthcoming. He implied that you knew much more than he did."

"About what?"

"Detective, we had an agreement, didn't we? It's beginning to feel like you don't trust me. I'm calling about the double murder at New City and the missing surgeon. What's his name, Schlecter?"

Ron stopped talking. Somehow, Edderman had gotten the name of the surgeon they were seeking out of Tom. He may have said more, but as Ron considered the circumstances, he realized there wasn't much else known about Schlecter, by the police or Tom.

"Listen, Edderman, our deal was we would let you know some things early, and you would help us keep a lid on things during the investigation. And then we would give you the full story at the end. We are just at the beginning and not ready for your involvement."

"I understand all that, detective. Is your search for Dr. Schlecter, 'surgeon of interest' a secret? It's not in the newspaper, yet. Are you holding back that information for a good reason?"

"We don't want him to know we are looking for him. At least not right now."

"And when you decide to let that information go public, you intend to call me first, don't you." Edderman's voice had a touch of snark.

Another significant pause occurred before Ron sighed into the phone and said, "OK. If we decide that information needs to get out, I'll call you. In the meantime, don't call me."

CHAPTER 36

Wednesday, April 6

Captain Thorason looked up when they entered his office. Instead of perusing paperwork until they were seated, he made eye contact with both Gene and Ron as they took seats in front of his desk. The eye contact was neither friendly nor hostile and certainly was not The Look. Nonetheless, both detectives felt impelled to move quickly into the presentation of their status in the New City murder investigation and not to dally with pleasantries.

Ron began, "As you know, the body dump out west on Baltimore looks like it is Terry Demming, the missing laboratory assistant of Schlecter's. We can't be certain because they ran over his head, but I found his wallet in the area, and his car was abandoned nearby. Darringer is also uncertain about the time of death, but she guesses it was at least a couple of weeks."

"Huh."

"Yeah, Gene and I figure that must have been the first murder."

Gene added, "With the head all crushed, we can't be certain about whether the manner involved throat slash on not. Darringer said she'd look for bone injury when she got to the post."

Ron picked up the narrative. "Still," he said, ' all the deaths are someone known to Schlecter and who might have been seen by him as having let him down. The lab tech might have been responsible for delayed results and loss of funding, the research guy didn't fight hard enough to retain the funding, and the anesthesia guy was associated with the death in the operating room that lost Schlecter his privileges."

"Huh."

"Certainly the mode of death, the throat slash, seems consistent with a killer who has surgical skills or familiarity. And probably access to surgical equipment, knives and all."

Gene added, "We still can't find Schlecter. Several reports about his car but none of them panned out. He's moving around, we think, and living off cash. Since we can't find him at any motel or hotel, we guess that he may be living in his car. Probably parks somewhere inconspicuous and moves it every day."

Captain Thorason nodded. Ron interpreted this as an indication that the Captain considered their idea about the car as habitat as new information, not yet arousing questions.

Ron spoke up after a brief lull in the conversation after Thor looked directly at him. "Of course, we're still looking for him locally but he may have gone far away. If all his revenge is over, he could have just gone anywhere. Tom said he had some kind of connection to laboratories on the West Coast."

"Huh."

"Right. We don't know that and we are staying on top of things here. We'll let you know more when we learn anything new."

Both detectives stood and turned toward the door. The Captain watched them leave without comment.

Back at their desks, Gene said, "Listen, it occurred to me that our visit to the gym where the good doctor had membership ended up with us talking to that guy who was filling in for the regular guy.

Ron scratched his chin and said, "He said he knew who Schlecter was and hadn't seen him."

"Right. But maybe he didn't see him because he wasn't there. The 'fill in' guy, I mean, not the doctor."

"Roger."

"You agree?"

"The guy's name was Roger," Ron said looking in his little notebook. "But, yes, I also agree that maybe he wasn't in the gym often enough for us to take his statement as proof that Schlecter really hadn't been there."

"So, I'm thinking maybe we ought to go back there in the morning and hit up the owner. He might have other information."

Ron nodded. "Might as well. I mean, we have no other leads right now, and I don't want to just sit around waiting for another BOLO report."

"The gym opens early for guys that want to hit the bag or something before work. I looked at their schedule on the bulletin board."

"OK. Let's meet here at six-thirty. We can be at the gym by seven."

CHAPTER 37

Thursday, April 7

They didn't make it to the gym. Ron insisted they take his car, and Gene wanted to get coffee and a doughnut before heading out. They made a quick trip to the coffee shop, but even so, they were only leaving the parking area when they got a call about another body at New City.

"Crap," Gene said. "There goes any chance he was finished."

"But it means he is still hanging around. That means we have a chance to catch him, partner."

They sped through traffic without using their siren and arrived at the scene in less than 10 minutes. Once again, officers directed them to the parking deck, but this time to one of the lower floors. As before, they located the taped area, parked several places away, and approached the cluster of people on foot.

A uniformed officer raised the tape for them to enter the scene. Ron asked him who was present and learned that Dr. Darringer was present and running the scene.

Looney approached where Darringer was kneeling next to a body. "Morning, doc," he said as he neared. "What've we got here?"

"A repeat offender, I'm afraid. This is Doctor Donald Piringa. Fifty-six-year-old male killed by a slashing knife wound to the left side of the neck. The cut severed the jugular and the carotid. Bled to death in a matter of minutes."

"Time?"

"My best estimate is around 12 hours ago. He's been lying here on the concrete in the cold night air, so I'm probably only going to get a several hour window."

"I don't see Tom."

"Oh, he was here, with Monique. The hospital is aware."

"Who found the body?" Gene asked, making his circuit around the corpse.

"Actually, one of the hospital security guards. The dead man left home after dinner last night to check on a patient. He was reported late and missing by his wife at midnight. She called the hospital and asked people to look for him, and they looked in his office and on the wards. Just before his shift ended, one guard decided to look in the garage."

"You sure this is like the others?"

"Look, detective, I'm getting to be an expert on this type of wound. And I'm sick and tired of it. You do your job and catch this maniac. I'll make the medical decisions."

"Don't get touchy, doc. I don't like this any more'n you. It's beginning to reflect rather poorly on our detecting ability."

"Sorry. I'm just tired. And I got called out of bed to come here. If you're done here, I'll move the body. Post this afternoon."

"Call if there's something for us to see."

"Oh, there'll be plenty to see. And you've seen it all before."

"OK, doc. How about calling us if there's something new?"

"Yeah. I'll do that." Darringer stood up and indicated to her assistants to move the body into the morgue van.

Gene and Ron stood together and watched the removal silently and then used their flashlights to check the immediate area for possible evidence. When they found nothing of help in the immediate area, they increased their search. They sought not only clues connected to the murder but also any sign of someone lying in wait.

Thirty minutes later, they huddled once again. "I got nothin'," Gene said. Ron nodded, "Yeah. I don't see anything either."

"This guy is either very disciplined to wait without giving any sign, or he's been incredibly lucky to find his target whenever he wants."

"Why is he hanging around the parking area? And how is it he keeps from being seen?"

They looked at each other for a moment and then said, almost simultaneously, "The car!"

"Right," Looney said. "He uses his card, gets in the parking lot, and waits for his target. Probably parks near to the target's car. We've been all over the city while he's been parking right here."

Gene wondered, "Maybe the gate system has a record."

"We'll check that. But right now, I want to find out from Tom what this dead guy had to do with Schlecter."

CHAPTER 38

Thursday, April 7

Tom Bolling was sitting in the morning meeting with a very nervous group of individuals. Roslyn asked Alena to present a report demonstrating that the "high number' of consults to the new Intermediate Care section was hampering direct nursing time and care of those patients. Tom asked to see the data, and Alena reluctantly gave him her notes. He pointed out that her notes did not contain the data she had mentioned. She looked at him blankly. Roslyn said, "The nurses collected that data on the ward, Doctor. Trust me, this is good data."

The discussion then turned from what the data might or might not indicate to 'trust'. That, of course, soon became a basis for raising the concept of 'handmaidens'. Sam intervened, finally, and asked about other issues.

Tom reported that the Flu Immunization program had only vaccinated 55% of the staff. Everyone shook heads and looked down at the table.

Sam brought up the murder in the parking deck and insisted that the security guards begin escorting anyone who parked there to their car, day and night. Tom pointed out that such action would not protect people coming into the hospital from the parking deck, and Sam became flustered.

"We've got to do something to protect our people from this maniac, Schlecter. I'll try posting a guard out there."

"That will probably help, Sam. Good idea."

Roslyn pointed out, "The nurses don't park there. That area is only for the doctors and the administrators. We need protection in our parking area, too. This man is deranged and no telling who he is looking to kill next."

Holly and Alena nodded vigorously at this, and Alena added, "I remember his temper. The nurses need escorts, too."

Tom was quick to add his agreement with that request, and immediately Sam began to waver because of the manpower involved.

"I don't know that we can do that for all shifts," he said. Both nursing executives stared at him. He swallowed and tried another tack, "Perhaps we could cluster everyone going at the same time and protect each other that way."

Tom intervened with, "Look, Sam, we either protect everybody or nobody. We are all at the same risk here." During the ensuing silence, he noted that Sam was sweating and the nurses were smiling at him. He went on, "I believe we can improve the safety in the parking areas all around the hospital with better lighting. And, we should ask folks to try to come and go in groups. Then, individuals can ask the security guard to walk them out if they are alone."

Sam was nodding through this presentation. He looked at the nurses and noted their nods, and so endorsed the plan. "That's good. Let's get some instruction out about the staying in groups, and I'll let security know what's expected of them."

When the meeting broke up shortly after, Sam was dictating a long memorandum to Holly addressed to Engineering and Security dealing with lighting and scheduling coverage in the parking areas.

Tom found Ron and Gene waiting for him in his office. Each had a cup of Green Bean coffee from the lobby kiosk and seemed to have made themselves at home.

"Mary let us in. She said we could wait in here," Ron explained as they both stood at his entrance.

"Hmmm," was Tom's reply.

"We need to get information about this latest dead guy. What was his relation to Schlecter?"

"Sit down. This is one Meluvahess, Ron, this 'dead guy' as you call him, was a revered cancer researcher and oncologist. His name is, I'm sorry, was, Donald Piringa."

"Uh-huh. OK, Dr. Piringa, it is. What was his connection to Schlecter?"

"Pretty straight-forward, I think. Don was the chair of the Research Committee. He would have been part of the decision to stop funding Schlecter's research."

CHAPTER 39

Thursday, April 7

The story on Dr. Piringa was, as Tom had said, pretty straight-forward. He had been on staff at New City for more than fifteen years after being recruited away from Cleveland Clinic to establish a Pediatric Oncology program at New City. Under Piringa's direction, that program had developed a national reputation and was heavily funded by research foundations, including the National Institutes of Health. Piringa, himself, was funded for two major clinical projects and was personally involved in the enlisting of patients and their ongoing care.

Four years before, the institutional research committee asked Piringa to take the chair. The responsibility involved setting up procedures to review all proposals that New City staff wanted to submit to funding agencies for review. Piringa had also established procedures of ongoing status review for all funded projects to assist researchers in staying current with their progress reports. He had also established the practice of 'sweeping' unobligated funding near the end of each quarter and using it to support other activities in the program. He brought that idea from its application in most research programs nationally and had minimal difficulty persuading researchers that the practice was best for the program. His point was that most funding agencies insisted that unobligated funds at the end of each quarter be returned to the agency. Piringa's practice was to keep the money locally.

According to his wife, Don Piringa had a deep commitment to patients included in either of his clinical studies. He often sat at their bedside and told stories or read Winnie-the-Pooh books to the patients after hours. It was this dedication that led him to leave home on the night of April 6 to visit a patient in the hospital. The patient was a six-year-old boy from Missouri, who had been particularly frightened by the technology of New City. Piringa had encouraged his parents to bring furnishings from his own bedroom to make things more familiar. He often went back to the hospital around bedtime to read to the boy.

He had left home shortly before eight o'clock after eating supper and told his wife he would be home by ten o'clock. She went to bed and fell asleep but awoke around one o'clock in the morning and realized he was not in the bed. She had gone through the house to see if he had come in and when he was not there she began texting and then calling him. By three o'clock in the morning, she called the police and reported him missing.

A pair of officers came to the house and interviewed her. They discovered he had gone to the hospital and called New City to speak to Security. At the request of the police, Security from New City looked throughout the facility including Piringa's office and his laboratory without success. Police visited the facility and talked with the parents of the boy from Missouri. They were staying in one of the respite rooms and had seen Piringa reading to their son around nine the previous evening. They had seen him leave the ward around nine-thirty. No one else was found to have seen him after that.

During an early morning discussion with Security, the police mentioned he had left the hospital around nine-thirty and one of the guards decided to check the parking area. Piringa had a reserved spot on the fourth deck but his car was not there. Sometime later the guard thought to check lower decks since parking there would put Piringa closer to the entrance than on the fourth deck. He found the car and Piringa's body and notified the police who were still at the hospital.

Ron and Gene reviewed the position of the body and the wounds on the neck and came to the same conclusion as Dr. Darringer: same method, probably the same killer. In fact, the mechanics looked the same. The target was likely about to get into the car when approached from behind. Apparently, the target was addressed and turned to speak with the killer before being struck with the slashing movement and falling to the ground.

"Gotta be someone he knew," Ron noted.

"He knew Schlecter."

"Yeah, but he also knew that Schlecter was considered dangerous. Why would he let him get that close?"

"Maybe he didn't hear him until the last second when he turned around."

"I don't think we can rule that out for this guy. But, remember, that anesthesia guy had put his briefcase in the car and turned around."

"But maybe he wasn't aware he should be afraid of Schlecter at that moment."

"OK. Maybe. I still have this mental Rembrandt of each victim being hailed, turning around and letting their killer get close enough to slash their throat in one swipe. It's unnerving, and I'm troubled."

Gene thought for a moment and then, "I'm troubled, too, partner. But I'm also hungry. I didn't get anything but the doughnut this morning. Let's go get lunch."

CHAPTER 40

Friday, April 8

The next morning they were still puzzling over the situation. The increasing number of murder scenes was not providing any additional clues or information about who was involved. And there was decreasing information about where that person might be. Looking at the gathering of negative information they had accumulated on where Dr. Schlecter had turned out not to be present, Gene had opined that they soon would be out of places to look for him in Cincinnati.

Their most recent trip to the coffee shop involved somewhat more hand-waving and frowning than usual. They agreed that in their present mood they shouldn't be discussing the case in a semi-public place. So, they were once again sitting across the desktops and talking, leaning forward to be heard in a quiet voice since they did not want to attract the Captain's attention.

Ron agreed with Gene's comment as they entered the Dick Pen, "You're right. We've got four murders on our hands now and not any progress since we caught the first one. I mean, if we don't count all the activity that proved Schlecter isn't anywhere around."

"I still think he's hanging around here somewhere," Gene commented as he sipped at his coffee. "I think the best evidence of that is the string of murders he keeps adding up."

"Don't remind me. That ongoing string suggests that he's not done yet, and we may soon be rolling to another site."

"The Captain agreed to put more patrols around New City at your request, so that might stop him."

"Or he'll move his activity to another place. I'm hoping if we can push him out of that parking deck, we'll have a better shot at ringing him up on the BOLO."

"Do you have the sense he is accelerating?" Gene asked, changing the subject.

"I think it certainly feels that way. But maybe that's because the first one wasn't found until recently."

Gene picked up a pencil and began doodling on a pad. "Let's see, the ME says Demming was killed around mid-March, and we know MacFarlane was killed on March 21. When was that anesthesia guy killed?"

Opening his Murder Book and thumbing quickly through the pages, Looney answered, "Finkbeiner. He was killed on March 27. And this last one, Piringa, was killed on April 6th."

"Let's see, then. That's six days between Demming and MacFarlane and six more till Finkbeiner."

"And nine or ten days until Piringa. Not really accelerating. We added Demming to the list just before we caught Piringa. That's why it seems to be accelerating."

"About Demming, has the doc said anything to you about the mode of death?"

"Haven't actually heard from her about that one at all."

"Well, it's only been a couple of days."

"Still. She might tell us something important." He reached out and picked up the phone.

When Darringer answered, Looney could hear the echo in the room and understood she was answering him hands-free. "Morgue. Darringer"

"Hey, doc. It's Looney. Gene and I were wondering if you found anything about a mode of death on Demming. I kinda thought you'd call us if it was another slashing."

"Well, that's probably true, Detective. But you may not be aware that I have several other cases that are, shall I say, more 'fresh'. And the detectives on those cases are standing right here. Shall I tell them to go away?"

"Hah! If I thought that would work, I'd say 'yes'. But we all know what homicide detectives are like."

Another voice from the speakerphone interjected, "Hang up, Looney. The doc is working our case and doesn't need distractions."

"Hey, Rocky. I recognize your voice. I really can't imagine a bigger distraction than you parading around the room. Maybe you should leave and let the doc do her work."

"Hang up, Looney."

Darringer interrupted. "I haven't gotten to Demming yet, detective. I'll let you know when it's scheduled." And the line went dead.

"Nothing, huh?" Gene asked.

"Well, for right now. But look. We know who it is and that he had a connection to Schlecter, just like the others. I doubt that finding a different mode of death will make me think any differently about Schlecter as our culprit."

"No, I wasn't thinking that either. Maybe our biggest break was figuring out that he must have been hiding out by living out of his car in the hospital parking deck. If we really have pushed him out in the open, the BOLO is gonna catch up with him, right?"

"I certainly hope so. We've checked the house. He's not there, and it looks like he bolted with clothes and suitcase gone. The financial guys say he pulled all that cash, and that looks like he's trying to stay off the grid. We know he hasn't been to his club or that gym. So by now, he's gotta be really stinky, or he's found a way to take showers."

Gene sat up straight and said, "Maybe we could get some bloodhounds to track him. Get some of his stinky socks from the house and let the dogs loose in Cincinnati."

Captain Thorason's comment surprised both of them since they were unaware he was standing nearby. "That won't be happening, Novalchek. But in the meantime, you two might want to check out an attack over at the medical school."

"What's that all about? Any connection to us?" Looney asked. He remembered how Thor had understood the connection of the construction body dump to their case very early.

Thorason looked at Looney steadily for a few seconds then said, "They called in an attack. Some guy pulled a knife on one of the doctors. Close enough for you?"

"Yes, sir. Knife attack on a doctor. That sounds very much like something we should be looking into. Right away. On the way." Looney said as he and Gene scrambled out of their chairs and grabbed their coats on the way to the stairs.

CHAPTER 41

Friday, April 8

Without comment, the two detectives moved swiftly to Looney's car and exited the garage. He turned on to E. Central Parkway and headed west, swinging north around the Washington Park area onto Highway 127. Traffic was moderate, and they moved around other vehicles without using the lights or the siren. Just before the big west turn toward the Interstate, Ron exited on Ravine and headed north. He took the right-then-left at McMillan on to northbound Clifton Avenue as Gene commented, "At least the University campus is quiet."

"Some think the death on campus during the time of the riots downtown made everybody a little more reserved."

"As if college students are ever reserved."

They stayed straight ahead at the circle with Martin Luther King and had Burney Woods on their right and Good Sam Hospital on their left as they proceeded north on Clifton to the Medical School Campus. A uniformed policeman at the entrance gave them directions to the parking garage near the administration building.

They saw the yellow tape as soon as they arrived on the second deck, and they parked nearby. Several individuals were standing around a parked car near the elevator bank, and they headed there. Ron flashed his badge and credentials as they approached and was recognized by the sergeant at the scene.

"Walker," the sergeant said with a nod.

"Brennan," Ron replied. "What do we have here?"

"This doctor was getting out of her car when she was attacked by a man with a knife." The sergeant indicated a tall, thin black woman in a long coat standing off to the side of the area.

"But not hurt?"

"No. He apparently hacked at her but dropped the knife and ran."

"Who is she?"

"Uh, she's a pediatrician and works at the medical school here," the sergeant referred to his notes. "Her name is Patrice Escobar."

"Thanks, Sergeant. We'll talk with her."

As they approached the woman, Ron saw her be at least five foot ten inches. She had a lean face of cafe au lait complexion, prominent lips, and striking eyes. She watched him approach but waited for him to speak.

"Dr. Escobar, I'm Detective Looney and this is my partner Detective Novalchek."

"Gentlemen," she acknowledged. Her voice was smooth and not agitated.

"Can you tell us what happened here?'"

"You are aware that I have already told your sergeant what happened?" she asked, not irritated or angry, just inquisitive.

Ron said, "Yes, ma'am. I am aware of that. I'm also remembering what an old doctor friend told me about reciting a history. It gets better the more often it is told."

"Smart guy. Anyone I know?" definitely interested.

"Tom Bolling at New City."

"I was right. Smart guy," she said, nodding and smiling at Ron.

Ron was impressed that this woman had recently survived an attempt on her life and was apparently completely calm about the experience. "Could you just tell me what happened?"

"Certainly. I pulled into the parking place here," she said, indicating that the closest car inside the tape was hers. "I opened the door and stepped out and then reached back inside to get my purse. I heard someone say my name and turned toward the rear and saw a man standing there. As I straightened up he said something like, 'you're all the same!' and swung a knife at me." She stopped at that point and Ron could see some increase n the wetness in her eyes.

"Why didn't he cut you with the knife?"

She paused and regrouped for a moment. "Well, he was chopping at me and I guess I blocked his arm with mine. And the purse."

"What happened then?"

"He saw he had dropped the knife and he turned and ran."

"Which direction?"

"Back toward the front gate.'

Ron gave her a moment to pause and then asked, "Did you recognize him?"

"Not really. I mean, he looked vaguely familiar, but I was focused more on the hand and the knife."

"Uh-huh. Can you describe him?"

"Somewhat. Indeterminate age White male, wearing blue jeans and a gray hoodie with the hood over his head and face. I think he was wearing running shoes. His feet impressed me as white as he ran away."

"Beard?"

"Ah, no."

"Glasses?'

"No."

"Hair?"

"Covered by the hood."

Ron stopped his questioning again and waited a moment. When she raised her eyes to look at him, he went on, "Are you aware that this man may have killed four other people?"

"The sergeant explained something about that when he said two men from Homicide would be coming to talk to me. Were these the physicians at New City?"

"Yes. From what we can piece together, the attacks on them were much as you described. Standing face to face, this man slashes his victims' throat with his right hand. One strike, and he walks away.'

Dr. Escobar looked at him without speaking.

He went on, "Can you tell me, doctor, how you managed to defeat that blow and disarm him?'

"You mean why aren't I dead like those others?"

"Yes. That's exactly what I want to know."

"No, I cannot. But there is one possibility."

"And that is …?"

"I am left-handed, detective. And I play a lot of squash. My husband says I have a better forehand than most men he plays against. My arm went up quickly and forcefully to defend myself when he tried to strike. Perhaps he didn't see that in his other victims."

"It's pretty clear he did not. Thank you, doctor." Ron turned back to review the scene and noted Gene leaning far under the vehicle next to Dr. Escobar's car. He came up wearing a surgical glove and holding a piece of blue plastic about the size of a popsicle stick.

"We can make one small change in our list of Knowns," Gene said, holding the item toward Ron. "This is definitely a surgical blade."

CHAPTER 42

Friday, April 8

They chose to sit at the corner table in the rear of the coffee shop, each with their back to a wall. Ron kept rubbing his eyes and Gene did a lot of staring over his partner's shoulder. They were avoiding the discussion that needed to be held. After a brief silence, Gene offered, "Well, I found me a tax guy."

"Good. Now you'll have more time to spend on the job."

"I wasn't spending time on my taxes."

"No, you were spending time worrying about taxes and searching for an accountant."

"Anyway, he said he'd have 'em done early next week."

"Plenty of time. Probably, he'll get them done quickly because they're easy."

Gene stuck his tongue out at Ron and took a drink of his cup.

Halfway through his cup of coffee, Ron started them back on topic of the murders with, "Escobar was not exactly what we expected."

Gene nodded, "Not at all."

"Nice lady. Pretty well composed with all that."

"But no contact with Schlecter."

"Well, she knows him. But apparently, they have only spoken at school functions."

"And only in passing. She says she cannot remember a real conversation between them."

"What's wrong with us, Gene? Why can't we figure this out?" More rubbing of the eyes followed this question. Gene obviously didn't have an answer, so he sat quietly and began to rub the bridge of his nose.

"Look," Ron finally said, leaning back in his chair. "I have got to believe that we are missing something." Gene nodded in agreement so Ron continued, "Unless this guy is just a total wacko trying to decimate the medical profession of Hamilton County, there's got to be a thread connecting these attacks."

"I agree, partner. But it is not startlingly evident."

"We gotta have some help on this and I see two possible ways for us to find a connection if there is one."

"Tell me. I got nothing."

Ron leaned forward to speak in a lower voice. "So far, everyone attacked has been in the medical profession. I think we need to have a sit-down with Tom to do some spit-balling."

Gene nodded. "And we can get a 'usual' at the coffee kiosk."

"You just finished a cup of coffee. Why are you thinking of more?"

"'Cause Nick's 'usual' is so much better."

"I'll give you that," Ron tossed off the last of his drink and started to rise. Gene put out his hand and said, "Wait a minute. You said you had two ideas. That's one. What's the other one?"

Ron smiled and said, "Let's talk to Tom first. Going to him seems to make the most sense, right now. The other idea I had was since the attacks were all medical, and involved people with connections to the medical school, maybe we should look there."

Gene looked at Ron and said, "I like that idea. Who do we talk to over there? This Dr. Escobar didn't seem to have any obvious connection."

"Yeah, I know. That's really bothered me, too. That's another thing I'm pretty sure that Tom will be able to advise us about. Who to talk to at the Medical School."

Gene said, "As I already said, I like the idea of New City and getting a 'usual' from Nick." He started whistling 'We're off to see the Wizard' as they headed for the door.

CHAPTER 43

Friday, April 8

As usual, Tom Bolling was a fount of information. He and the two detectives sat in his office for a couple of hours brainstorming ways in which the individuals killed and Patrice Escobar might have been associated.

Tom had started by mentioning all the various activities that the New City victims might have had in common. As he explained the daily activity of the individuals, starting with Schlecter himself, Ron and Gene took copious notes.

"First," Tom said, "there's the basic job itself. A surgeon has three areas of 'practice' if you will. He, or she, initially sees most patients on a referral as an outpatient. So the contact would be in the surgeon's office. That would bring a patient into contact with office personnel, office assistants like nurses and physician assistants as they are registered and prepared to see the surgeon."

"You mean like getting weighed and having their blood pressure taken?" Gene asked.

"Right. Then the surgeon comes in and talks to the patient, getting a history of what ails them. And then does the relevant physical exam."

"Everybody gets undressed, right?" Looney wanted to know.

"Well, not always and not completely undressed usually. Why?"

"I don't know. I just thought maybe something might go on with them being undressed and that would cause resentment."

"Well, all such examinations are chaperoned. So I don't think that's a likely cause."

"Okay."

"Then the patient is scheduled for surgery. That might be in a hospital if it's a big case but more surgery is done now in an ambulatory surgery center."

"How does that work?" Gene asked. "I always wondered how you could operate on somebody walking around."

"That's not what the 'ambulatory' means, Gene. I think you're pulling my leg."

"A little."

"Ambulatory surgery means you get up and 'walk out' after it's over. No hospital stay or even overnight. This concept was one of the real disruptions to medical practice back in the 1970s and 80s."

"Meaning?" Ron inquired.

Well, until then all surgery was done with the patient admitted to the hospital and using the operating room in the hospital. That cost a lot of money, just the personnel to handle all the details ran the cost up. Plus hospital space is expensive to use."

"So the ambulatory thing …?"

"Created a big disruption for hospital income. Many minor cases, and now even larger cases like joint replacements are done in the ambulatory setting."

"Did Schlecter do that? The ambulatory thing?"

"Yes. Sometimes. Like most hospitals, we have an ambulatory surgical center attached to our inpatient care facility. He did cases there when it was appropriate."

"Could he have done something inappropriate and cause all this trouble?"

"Not likely. We still have all the safeguards for patients. The only real difference is we are working in a much cheaper environment."

"But that's only part of what he would have been doing, right?"

"Yes. Schlecter had operating room privileges and also worked with inpatients. That was where he had his problem."

That comment led Tom into a discussion of the credentialing and privileging mechanism within hospitals to assure everyone that physicians practicing in the hospital had requisite training and experience for procedures or treatments that they did. He briefly told them about the death in the operating room and how Schlecter had lost his privileges. That helped the detectives understand how Schlecter would have felt - as if they were told they could no longer wear a badge or carry a weapon.

Tom went on to explain the day-to-day activities of a practicing surgeon: early morning rounds to see hospitalized patient previously operated on, scrubbing in for one or more cases in the operating room, checking on the inpatients and tests ordered then hurrying to an office to see several more patients to schedule for surgery and then making late afternoon or evening rounds back in the hospital. Looney said he got tired just hearing that schedule. Gene wondered when they had time to eat.

But the real eye-opener for the detectives came when Tom started explaining the activities attendant upon having an academic appointment. All the other tasks of patient examination, treatment, and follow-up were unchanged. However, academia had additional requirements for physicians. Since they were usually drawing some remuneration from the medical school for their appointment, each physician was expected to serve on hospital and medical school committees. As Tom gave examples of these committees, both detectives began to roll their eyes.

Record review committee work, Quality Assurance activity, working on the Utilization Committee each sounded like a potential career in itself. Then Tom explained that the medical school wanted the doctors to be a part of the Curriculum Review Committee, the Student Advancement Committee, and even such intense endeavor as the Appointment and Promotions committee or interviewing potential medical school candidates. Tom also explained that the academic career ladder and the criteria reviewed by the Promotions committee involved individuals being engaged successfully in scientific advancement - research, publications, and obtaining funding from outside the school for their activities.

"Now I want to know when these guys sleep!" Gene said.

"And that's not all, really," Tom continued. "Most of the really successful ones are members of various national organizations like Alpha Omega Alpha or some specific research or clinical group connected to their work, such as the Midwest Oncology Group. Those organizations also want some time commitment from members."

"Geez," Ron said. "Do we have to check and cross-check all those organizations to find where our victims overlap?"

"Along with any social clubs or local organizations they may have joined."

Gene looked at Looney and raised his eye heavenward.

"Ron said, "We intended also, to find out what someone like Schlecter might be doing for the medical school. Did you mention everything?"

"As far as I know. You can check with the Dean to be sure."

"Yeah. That's what we want. Someone there."

Tom opened the top drawer on his desk and pulled out a card. "Her name is Janet Wisener. Here's her card with contact information. Tell her I sent you, and she'll probably provide coffee."

"As good as our 'usual'?" Gene asked.

"Probably not. But it will come in a china cup with a saucer."

CHAPTER 44

Monday, April 11

Looney had called ahead and made an appointment for them to meet with the Dean. He and Gene were a few minutes early since they had to locate her office at the medical school. Turned out the signage was very adequate and they easily found the meeting place. The Office of the Dean was a large, open space at one corner of the administration building. The far wall of the office was a solid window forty feet long looking into the building entrance quadrangle. The large office area contained eight desks occupied by young people, men and women, each working diligently at some task. One in the far corner recognized their arrival and stood to greet them.

"Are you the detectives?" she asked.

"Yes, M'am, I'm Detective Looney and this is my partner Detective Novalchek."

"Nice to meet you. I'm Shirley Whittleston, the Dean's secretary. Dean Wisener asked that I let you in her office. She will be here shortly." She turned to open a door behind her desk and ushered the detectives into a dark-paneled office lined with bookshelves. There was a small desk near the window and a small two-cushion sofa with two wingback chairs surrounding a small glass-topped table centrally placed in the room. Shirley indicated they could pick a seat.

"Would you like coffee or tea?" she asked.

Both men indicated they would, and she turned to go, leaving the door open.

"This is a lot more impressive than that corner office of Thor's," Gene noted looking around at all the books.

"She probably pulls down a more impressive salary than he does, too," Ron said taking one of the wingback chairs.

"Kinda small desk for such an important job, I think."

"You never know. Maybe all her desk work is ceremonial."

"Wouldn't that be cool? I could get behind that. No riding around in your car with the broken seat springs, no walking the neighborhoods …"

"My car seat springs are not broken."

"Then it's the suspension. Whatever. No more of that nonsense, and …"

Shirley returned at that moment with their coffee. As predicted, they were each presented with a china cup on a saucer. Shirley brought the cups on a silver tray that also held sugar and cream in small silver containers. Both men took their cups and indicated they did not need the sugar or cream. Shirley again mentioned that the Dean would be down presently and left, again leaving the door open.

"Well, Tom was right about the china," Gene noted, sipping at his cup. "And it's good and hot, and really tasty. Is that cinnamon?"

"I think so. Maybe we could start adding cinnamon to the pot in the office."

"It might just catch on fire. But this is good coffee."

A woman's voice from the open doorway interrupted him. "I'm so glad you like it. It's one of my special blends from Vienna."

They turned and stood to greet Dean Wisener. She was a striking figure of perhaps five foot seven in height with a bright face and smile that made them want to smile back. Her dark hair was worn in a modified pageboy cut and swirled with her head movement. Her gray eyes looked out from half-glasses on her nose. "Please sit down. I've asked Shirley to bring me some coffee, but let's get started on why you're here."

Impressed with the Dean's 'get-down-to-business attitude, Ron began by giving Wisener the briefest of details about the four known murders and the similarities between those and the attack earlier on Dr. Escobar. During his presentation, Shirley quietly entered, placed the Dean's coffee in front of her on the table, and left, closing the door behind her. The Dean nodded her awareness of the coffee but did not take her eyes off Ron as he spoke.

Ron felt that the Dean was somehow already up to speed on his presentation and he quickly came to his reason for visiting. "We initially thought the connection between the murders existed at New City but the attack on Dr. Escobar made us pause to consider …"

"Whether the pool of victims might be infinitely larger," the Dean interjected.

"Well, yes. Or, said another way, whether some thread connects these people through the medical school instead."

"Will you give me their names again?"

"Certainly," Ron said as he handed her the list of victims, including Patrice Escobar.

The Dean called Shirley and gave her directions of seeking the academic enrollment folder for each of the individuals on Ron's list. While she was carrying out that search, the Dean turned to the detectives and asked, "Is there anything, in particular, you would like to know."

Gene commented, "What are all those people working on in your office?"

Dean Wisener laughed gently at his question. "Yes," she said, "many people wonder just what I do all day. The Office of the Dean has multiple responsibilities that most people don't think about. First, the Office has responsibility for the medical school starting with recruiting students, interviewing them, and admitting them, then managing their advancement through prescribed coursework and certifying them for graduation as able to sit for their Board."

"That sounds like it would take a lot of time."

"Well, yes, it does. There are some associate Deans with major responsibilities in particular areas but this Office coordinates and certifies everything."

"Big job," Gene agreed.

"And it's only one of the jobs I do." She went on, "I also have responsibility for hiring the chairs of the various departments in the school and seeing that they have sufficient funding to do their job."

Ron actually shuddered at the thought of such a responsibility. He wanted only to have a clear picture of what was expected of him and to have others stay out of his way. Under no circumstances did he want a series of people reporting to him and him responsible for how they did their job.

The Dean went on, "Plus, there's the issue of post-graduate education, as well"

"Is that something we're going to have to understand in depth?" Ron asked.

"I don't know. It will depend somewhat on what Shirley finds in those folders." As she was speaking, the door opened, and Shirley entered, handing the Dean the requested folders.

Over the next half hour, the Dean took Ron and Gene through a short course in medical school activities. She reviewed each of the individual folders and showed the detectives how each individual had served on various committees over the years, occasionally as chair, most often as a member. When they completed the review, Ron noted that the targeted medical school faculty had served together on only one committee and then only for one year and that was three years previously. Gene thought that did not constitute a break-through, and he said so.

Ron thanked the Dean and prepared to leave. She noted the degree to which her information had deflated each of them and said, "This may not be the only way these people shared an experience, you know."

"Oh," Ron inquired. "What else is there?"

"Well, each department also asks the faculty to get engaged in teaching the students at various times. The new curricula call for clinical correlation between the basic sciences and the practice of medicine. Each department has a group of clinical faculty to help with that kind of teaching."

"Do you know who those individuals are?"

"Not specifically. Some are known to me but just a few. The lists are maintained by the departments."

"Any other good news?" Ron asked, the edge in his voice evident.

"Well, most of us on the faculty have served to interview prospective medical students and give them advice."

"Do you have a record of that involvement?"

"Probably not. Most of us run into prospective students while presenting at conferences or judging at Science Fairs or what-not. I do a little interviewing at times if someone actually makes an appointment and comes to the school. But most of the time, the faculty just pick it up on the fly."

Chapter 45

Monday, April 11

Looney called Tom from the car. They discussed the lack of any solid connection shared by all the victims, and Ron asked for a favor. He had been worried about the connection of Finkbeiner to the operative death and asked Tom to pull the cases where Schlecter and Finkbeiner had worked together. Tom asked Beverly to do so; they all agreed to meet right after lunch at New City.

Lunch was largely a repeat of every day for the past month. The detectives arrived and chose to sit in one of the booths at the front of the café. They lingered over their menus until Sandy came to take their order. She and Gene engaged in a little flirting and generally ignored Ron's presence. After they agreed to, once again, settle for their 'usual', Sandy walked off to put their order in, and both men watched her appreciatively.

"Still think we're gawking. And it's obvious," Ron said.

"Nobody is noticing us, partner. Everyone is watching my girl walk away."

"Well, I gotta say, you've got that going for you."

"Yes, I do."

"And to think how much I had to push you to ask her for a date."

"I was being polite and respectful."

Ron snorted, "Respectful! The way you watch her walk is anything but respectful. It's almost lustful."

"Appreciative, then."

"Whatever. I doubt that Thor will be appreciative about us coming up with another dry hole at the medical school."

"It may not be dry. There's a ton of opportunities for everyone to be connected across all those committees and organizations and stuff."

"And we will both qualify for retirement before we get through the potential connections. And I'm feeling that even then, we might not have an answer."

Gene nodded and sipped his iced tea. Ron looked at his hands. They sat quietly for a moment.

When Sandy brought their orders, she asked, "Everything all right, boys? You're not talking like usual."

"We're thinking," Gene explained as Ron nodded.

"Well, whatever you're doing, it looks like you don't do it very often, 'cause it hurts. Smile and enjoy your food!" And she walked away, again drawing their attention.

As they ate, Ron mused, "Sandy's right. I haven't had to think so hard about a case in a long time."

Gene added, "You know, I read somewhere that sugar is the fuel of the brain."

Ron looked at him quizzically. "How does that help us?"

"Well, I think today we should get some pie."

They did get pie, key lime for Gene, and cherry for Ron. But, again, as usual, they did not get coffee. After Gene took care of giving Sandy their money and chatting while Ron brought the car to the front of the café, they went directly for coffee at New City.

"I kinda like that Nick thinks we have a 'usual' here," Gene allowed as they entered the lobby and approached the coffee kiosk.

"But it could bode poorly for the hospital that a couple of homicide dicks are hanging around that often."

"Whatever, he makes a good cuppa."

Beverly joined them in Tom's office. The detectives knew that she was an important part of the decision-making in the hospital. Beyond that, they wanted her input. Ron knew she considered herself an administrator and not a clinician, and her insight into processes and personnel had been helpful to them in the past.

The detectives greeted Beverly by tipping their cups toward her and took their seats. Tom had a printout from the electronic medical record that he showed to the assembly and said, "Bev found only seven cases in the past three years where Finkbeiner was the anesthesiologist for a case performed by Adam Schlecter. All cases went as expected and, except for that last one, no complications. Every patient walked out of the hospital."

Ron thought to himself, 'I wish we had started keeping score on the things that didn't work out. We could have had a party by now.' He asked, 'Is there any other connection between him and Schlecter? Are we missing something and just settled on that bad operation because it was recent?"

Tom and Beverly shook their heads, and Beverly shrugged her shoulders and commented, "There certainly could be. They were both connected to the Surgical Service. They would have bumped into each other in the doctors' lounge and dressing room. They would have seen each other in the halls. They didn't need to have a common patient to interact."

"Well, we do have a connection and some friction between Schlecter and MacFarlane. And probably with Demming. What about this Piringa? What's his connection to Schlecter?"

Tom spoke to that question. "As I told you earlier, Don Piringa was a pediatric oncologist and was the chair of our in-house Research committee. I'm not aware that he and Adam shared any patient care. But Don would have been in a position to block or at least appeal the loss of Adam's research funding. He actually supported Adam's appeal for funding continuation."

"So, why would Schlecter would have seen him as working against him?"

"I don't know. The appeal was denied. We don't have any evidence that Adam ever said anything about Don working against him."

"And we don't have anything from the medical school connection to link Schlecter to the attack on Patrice Escobar."

Tom said, "I heard about that. Was she hurt?"

"No. In fact, she probably got off the best. Knocked the knife out of his hands."

"Was it Adam? Did she identify him?"

"No. She said, 'White guy in a hoodie'. Not really courtroom identification level."

Tom spoke again, "I'm really sorry we can't lay out a clear case of motive here. Schlecter had a niche here and pretty much stayed in it. After we lifted his surgical privileges, he spent a lot of his time in his research lab."

"And we got nothing from the lab girl. Bonnie Phillips. She's out in Los Angeles now. Didn't even know about some of the events. In her opinion, Schlecter was a bit of a mess but not a killer."

Beverly asked, "Did you talk to the young man in the lab?"

"I guess you don't know. It looks like he was the first person killed. We found his body in a construction site west of here last week."

"Oh, that's terrible. Are you suspecting Dr. Schlecter for that, too?"

"I don't see why not. He disappears, and there's a string of murders connected to him. Seems like a slam dunk."

"I thought you said you didn't have connections between Dr. Schlecter and some of the attacks. Like Dr. Escobar."

"Well, yes, technically, we don't have those connections right now. We are still looking."

Tom indicated he had to go to another meeting and said, "You know you're both always welcome to come to check on things here at New City. Even if we can't find that connection, we've got Nick, and he'll make you a 'usual'."

Chapter 46

Monday, April 11

The end of the day had come, but they had made no further progress in either understanding motivation or in locating Adam Schlecter. Sitting in the office after everyone else had left, Gene wanted to run through the list of 'Knowns' again. Ron was less interested but finally agreed with the provision that they would write down uncertainties and possibilities as well.

Gene started with, "Nothing has changed on number one, right?"

"Write it down, and let's see."

"Everyone killed had a link, maybe a close link, to Dr. Adam Schlecter."

"That's apparently not true for the attack on Dr. Escobar."

"I said, 'Everyone killed'. I still don't know what to do with her attack."

"Well, we're gonna have to put it on the list somewhere."

"I'm leaving number one the way it is, and moving to number two. There is good reason to believe that everyone killed had let Schlecter down in some way."

"Hold on a minute. Are we sure that's the reason for Finkbeiner's murder?"

"You got another reason?"

"No. But can we call that one a possibility rather than a 'Known'?"

"Okay. Can we agree that the method of killing involved a surgical blade and surgical-like skill? That hasn't changed, has it?"

"No, it hasn't. But that brings up the knife attack on Escobar and muddies everything."

"You want to leave her out of the reasoning?"

"Can't. Everything about the attack on her screams it was done by the person who killed the others."

"Yeah, I agree. Maybe we should change number one to say, All the attacks involved a knife and surgical-like skill."

"I like that. Then number two is we don't know the link between all the different people who were attacked and Schlecter."

Gene thought that over for a few seconds. "I don't like writing down that our number two 'known' is an unknown."

"All right, then. Don't. But the Escobar attack takes the connection of everyone to Schlecter less real to me."

"I'm going to say that number two on the list of 'Knowns' is most everyone who was attacked had a connection to a missing surgeon. How's that?"

Ron nodded. "I still don't think we have that information for Escobar. But, that's a fair way to keep us looking for Schlecter."

"Number three is that Schlecter has effectively disappeared, and that is very suspicious."

"I sure agree with that. He has to have seen the coverage in the newspaper and on television. He would have to be in a coma to miss it. And if he saw it and didn't come forward, he goes to the top of the suspect list."

"And we know he hasn't come forward."

They looked at each other for a moment savoring a degree of enrichment in their list. Then Ron said, "You know, there is one way that we might get Escobar to fit into this run of killings."

Gene put down his pen and put his hands behind his head. "And what's that, counselor? Is this your S.O.G. theory of the day? I always think that lawyers have run out of viable considerations when they turn to that old trick."

"No, I'm not going to suggest that the killings were done by Some Other Guy. I'm suggesting that the lack of connection may be the key."

"Random killings, you mean?"

"Well, somewhat random. Think about this. What if the killer really has only one person he wants to kill? There isn't a better way to hide that single killing than in a series of killings that all look alike. There's no real connection between these random people, so the police spend all their effort trying to find one. Meanwhile, the motive for the one intended killing is just buried under piles of extraneous facts and may be missed by the police."

Gene shook his head. "That sounds almost as far-fetched as S.O.G. There's really only one attack that doesn't have a connection to the same person - the missing surgeon, Schlecter."

"Which may mean that Dr. Escobar was the primary target all along."

"Are you suggesting a racial motive?"

"I'm trying to suggest that there's a lot we don't know, and motive for anything is still speculative."

"Or, it may mean that the primary target of this surgical-like killer is not yet been attacked."

"Or it could be that."

"You know you are blowing our list of 'Knowns' up completely, don't you. If we head off the way you're suggesting, we're going to have to alibi everybody in the hospital and the medical school. I can't see that happening."

Ron sighed. "You're right. Thor would never approve going after that broad a swath of uncertain guilty parties."

"Returning to the question of connection or maybe commonality, here's what I had written down earlier. We've got two cases tied directly to medical research, maybe a third with Piringa."

"You're counting Demming and MacFarlane?"

"And there's only one connected to the operating room. That's Finkbeiner."

"Agreed."

"Escobar, Finkbeiner, and Piringa have regular teaching activities and are active in medical school committees. That's three with medical school connections."

"You know those areas overlap to a significant degree, don't you?"

"Well, yes, but I was just trying to bring a new way of looking at these killings."

"We certainly need that, partner. But has your approach addressed the burning question?"

"You mean, 'where is Schlecter?' No, it doesn't."

"That question makes me think deep down that he is the link. I'm not gonna feel like we are making progress until we figure out where he went."

"Tom keeps mentioning that he told Schlecter to take some time off."

"Yes, he did. People like Schlecter in academia sometimes do that. It's called a sabbatical. They usually go somewhere to work on a major book or work in someone else's laboratory to gain some new skills."

"How do you know so much?"

"I talked to Tom about it and asked where Schlecter would go if he did take the sabbatical."

"I bet he didn't have any idea."

'Not taking that bet. Already know the answer."

"And what are we gonna do with the idea that these murders may be covering up the one murder that our killer has been planning all along. Which one do you think it is?"

"Why would it have to be one we've already run across? This killer may be planning a few more and may not have even killed the person he's after yet."

"That will keep me up all night."

"C'mon, Gene. You've been telling me that Sandy is keeping you up all night."

"Yeah, well. Not tonight. I need to sleep and ponder."

Ron stood and grabbed his coat in agreement with his partner. "This conversation didn't help me very much, Gene. Now my brain hurts. Let's go home."

CHAPTER 47

Monday, April 11

As soon as he opened his front door, Looney's spirits rose. He could smell dinner cooking. It was the special dinner that he recognized. For years after their marriage, Meg had understood Ron's need to spend an evening with "J.J. and John" but she was not happy about that involving him sitting in some jazz bar until closing time. They had several long discussions about how he might accomplish the needed reverie in a manner more acceptable to her.

Meg finally decided that she needed to create that environment for him at home. She encouraged him to collect albums of his favorite artists, J.J. and John and many others. She also talked up his thoughts about setting up speakers to play his albums and was most supportive when he began seeking a plain old turntable. They both were surprised at the dearth of such equipment in electronics stores and even in the second-hand market. Ron had spent more than four months searching through newspaper advertisements, internet offerings, and neighborhood rumors before he got what he wanted. It was a plain turntable with both 33 and 78 rpm settings. It came without a pre-amplifier, but Looney overcame that with built-in pre-amps in his speaker system.

Meg wasn't finished when the sound system was installed, however. She wanted to create an environment for Ron to make his new 'consultation arena' comfortable and effective. She decided that the best way to do that was to prepare his favorite meal for the evening before his 'consultation'.

Ron Looney had always considered fried chicken as his favorite. Not just fried but deep-fried. With thick, rich crust and moist hot meat, Ron thought there couldn't be a better meal. He thought it also required green beans, preferably cooked with a little fatback, mashed potatoes, and cornbread. So, Meg began making this meal whenever she determined that Ron had come to that point in an investigation where he needed 'consultation'. Over the past several years, they made a habit of certain parts of the evening. Results were best if Meg decided when to create the favorite meal. Ron requested the dinner one time, and that did not go well. Now the decision was all hers. Second, they ate the meal talking about other issues and topics but not his concerns about the case. An important third step included the dessert. She always prepared a fresh, hot apple pie and put a thick slab of cheddar cheese on his piece, served with a fresh cup of coffee.

The last part of their customary activities came with the cleanup. Ron brought all the dishes to the sink, and they stood together washing and drying them. They started that part of the ritual before they had the fancy electric dishwasher, and so it continued. They stood at the sink, side-by-side, touching at shoulder and hip until they had the dishes washed, dried, and in the rack. Then, they sat at the table discussing Meg's plans for the evening over a last cup of coffee.. She arranged that part of the evening, too. She usually made a trip to the library and picked up something by an author she liked. She would read in bed until she fell asleep.

When they finished that final cup of coffee, Meg took the cups to the sink and rinsed them out. She kissed the top of his head and left him sitting at the dining room table. Alone, Looney took a deep breath and started his routine. He rummaged through his collection and chose a couple of initial albums with plaintive melodies to fit his mood and put them on the turntable. He would end the evening with instrumentals, but he wanted to start with some vocals that he knew and loved. First, he put on a Billie Holiday album with 'Willow Weep for me', and 'Am I Blue?' He followed that with a Dexter Gordon album featuring "Chan's Song'. He set the volume low, ostensibly to keep from bothering Meg. The reality was, Ron didn't particularly like loud music.

He circled back into the kitchen, grabbed a beer from a cold six-pack, and sat on the couch, placing his papers on the coffee table. He had some notes he had taken at every interview, the list that he and Gene had discussed, and a folder of information about every person he had contacted in the case. He had brought the Murder Book home with him, as well. So he had the photos of scenes and the depositions of witnesses and other officers. Ron's practice during this 'consultation' was to re-read every entry. He wanted to be certain he remembered the facts correctly, then he would construct a putative timeline in his head that would explain the discrepancies and fill in the missing information.

An hour later, he found himself without beer. He went back to the refrigerator for a second bottle and resumed his reading. Two bottles later, he was finished reading. The timeline in his head appeared to have no starting point, however. He still had no idea on a motive, and the one they had started with seemed frayed and ill-fitting to some of the cases. Looney got up and paced around the living room before hitting the refrigerator for a piece of cold chicken. He ate the chicken standing and leaning against the sink counter, staring into space. Then he cleaned his hands and returned to put some different music on the turntable.

Looney was thumbing through the albums, and his eye was caught by an album featuring Hank Mobley. It included 'There's a Small Hotel' and 'All the Things you Are'.; he put that on the turntable. On top of that he placed an old favorite, 'Jazz Night in America' highlighting Wynton Marsalis with the Lincoln Center Orchestra. Then grabbed the fifth beer and sat down to reconsider his papers.

Shortly after midnight, Looney thought he might have an idea about 'who' but couldn't quite put it into words. He leaned back against the couch and closed his eyes to better 'see' his timeline. Within two minutes he was sound asleep.

He awoke for a call of nature hearing the plaintive strains of the flutes in 'Never and Forever'. On his way back from the toilet he opened the refrigerator and discovered he had finished the six-pack. He returned to the couch and tried to reconstruct the timeline. His difficulty came in pairing events on the timeline with people and a rational motive. He didn't want to go back to sleep and tried to keep from it by sitting upright on the couch but his head kept drifting downward. Twenty minutes later he was leaning back, eyes closed again, his vision of the whiteboard shaking with all the entries on it falling off. Then new pieces flew in from somewhere and stuck on the board … and they made a difference … and almost made sense …

But then he was asleep and stayed that way until Meg came down in the morning.

Chapter 48

Gene was sitting at his desk thumbing through his notes when Looney arrived the next morning. He had grabbed a breakfast sandwich and coffee on his way into the office, but that had been an hour before. Gene wondered where his partner was and avoided going anywhere near the Captain's office so he couldn't be asked. He was not particularly worried about Ron's absence at the beginning of the day. Both men often ran little side trips and relied on each other for cover. They would alert each other if needed in the office. Nonetheless, when Ron walked in with a beaming smile and, more importantly, two cups of coffee from the shop down the block, Gene was both relieved and pleased.

Gene grinned his approval and acceptance of one of the cups, "Why do you look like the guy with all the answers?"

"It was 'consultation night', partner. And the jazz artists did it again!"

"Tell me! I'd like to be there on one of those 'consultations' to see what actually goes on. Is it like some kind of séance? Ouija boards and voices from the closet kind of stuff?"

"None of that, man. Just good old hard work. And a fresh six-pack of Over The Rhine."

"What's so hard about that? Meg feeds you that special dinner you go on about, and then you sit in the living room and drink beer. I think a Ouija board would make more sense."

"This is why scientists have so much difficulty explaining things to farmers."

"Why? Because we're all dumb yokels?"

"Nope. It's all in the vocabulary. Jazz speaks a language I can hear and partially understand, that's all. Things that are disruptive or seem unharmonious sometimes just settle in to their place in that atmosphere."

"Okay, professor Brubeck, what did you figure out?"

"Well, it's not all crystal clear, but I think we have been a little off base from the beginning. Let me see if I can take you there."

"You bought the coffee. You get the floor."

"So, right from the beginning, from the MacFarlane murder, what did we suspect?"

"Uh, killing done in anger, probably because of the loss of research funds."

"Right. And that meant we began to focus on who might be the angry one. And that took us to Adam Schlecter."

"You are correct, sir. Rightly so, I might add."

"Hold on to your addition, you may need subtraction in a minute," Ron said before taking a long pull on his cup. "And the next thing was what?"

"We tried to find Schlecter."

"The next murder, I mean. C'mon, Gene, stick with me here."

"Okay. The next murder was Finkbeiner."

"And …"

"And we tied that to Schlecter because of the death in the operating room."

"Right. That's exactly what we did. But the woman died from what Tom told us was a clear-cut surgical error. It had nothing to do with the anesthesia. Why would Schlecter go after the sandman and not someone with their hands in the operation?"

"We talked about that. I recall we thought it was too hard to get to the resident or maybe Schlecter thought the anesthesia guy could have done more to help him. I guess. Why?"

"What if that's not the reason Finkbeiner was killed at all?"

"Well, I don't know. 'Cause I can't think of another reason that ties to MacFarlane."

"Neither could I until last night. Let me go on. At this point, all I want you to do is to agree that possibly we don't have a connection between the two murders. That's all."

Gene nodded, "I can try."

So Ron went on, "My next question is, 'Why was the next killing the guy on the research committee?' I mean we started with a research motive, then jumped to the operating room. Why now go back to research for a motive?"

"Stop a minute, here, Ron. You're giving me a bigger headache than one cup of coffee will cure. I remember we talked ourselves into a blanket motive that Schlecter was taking people out who had let him down. He had lost his operating privileges, and then he lost his research. He was itching for someone to blame for everything. That covers the research and the loss of funding and the death in the operating room, right?"

"Actually, that is right. That was exactly the reasoning we used. It's just wrong. I mean, we did come to that conclusion, but now I think we were wrong."

"You think there was some other motive for killing Finkbeiner? Are we sneaking up toward an S.O.G. theory or is this the serial killings to cover up a single murder motive?"

"None of the above, Gene. Just remember what Tom said about Schlecter and Piringa. He said Piringa supported his appeal about funding loss. And Tom said he had never heard Schlecter mention that he thought Piringa had acted against him."

"Yeah, but that doesn't mean he didn't come to that conclusion at some time."

"Yeah, I agree it's not a certainty. But I've really got some doubts here, and you haven't heard them all."

"Here I sit, patiently waiting."

"Well, at this point we either have a surgeon who is completely off his nut, making up motives to kill people he worked with, so unhinged that the motives are not tightly held together … or we have a diabolically thoughtful killer, able to hide in plain sight and get next to his victims even when they are warned about him."

"Huh."

"Right. That's exactly what Thor would say. And he would be right. The two pictures don't jibe. They're like pieces from two different jigsaw puzzles."

"What are you thinking, then?"

"Again, it's not completely clear, yet. But if we put things together this way, then the attack on Dr. Escobar may be the answer rather than a disconcerting fact that we can't explain."

"What do you mean?" Gene had finished his coffee and put both hands on top of his head. "The answer. I don't see an answer."

"C'mon, partner. We need to get that list of your's out and look at everybody on it for new connections. I think you were on the right track yesterday and neither of us could get off our first impression. We have been trying to force later information into our original mold rather than assess it fairly."

"What were you drinking last night? You wanna get us run out of the department?"

"I'm just saying. Better if you and I get this straight before someone else does, right?"

"I would agree with that as a goal. But I haven't yet seen where all your theories are going."

"Can't blame you for that. Try this on: not everybody attacked or killed had a connection to Adam Schlecter. But they all had some kind of connection to the medical school. I think that's where we need to start over, partner."

CHAPTER 49

Tuesday, April 12

Captain Thorason came out of his office shortly before noon. He saw Gene and Ron standing at Ron's desk as they pored over two stacks of records. They weren't talking and were diligent in their reading. So diligent, in fact, they did not hear him approach. He noted they were reviewing notes and personnel folders from the serial murder cases and decided to determine what they were up to.

"New information?" he asked, causing each of them to jump slightly.

"Ah, no, sir. Not exactly, new information," Ron said. "We're trying a new way to look at things."

"Huh."

"Absolutely. It definitely wasn't working the other way we were looking at things. We think there's a better way to put some of this together, now."

"Would you like a briefing, Cap'n?" Gene asked. Ron gave his partner a sidelong glance from under his colliding eyebrows, but the damage had been done.

"Sure. Come in the office."

"Let us get this stuff together, and we'll be right there," Gene said.

As the Captain walked back to his office, Ron stood with his arms folded and stared at Gene.

Gene shrugged and commented, "Had to happen sooner or later. I think you got good ideas here, and they'll make more sense if we convince Thor that we know what we're doing."

They gathered their material and spent three minutes outlining an approach to a presentation to the Captain. Recognizing that he had forced Ron's hand, Gene suggested they run to the coffee shop and bring a cup back for the Captain. Ron vetoed the idea, pointing out that the shop would be crowded close to lunchtime and that the Captain was waiting.

They took seats in front of the Captain's desk, and he folded his hands in his lap to listen to their presentation.

Ron decided that he would do the bulk of the presentation since most of the ideas came from his night of 'consultation'. Without an explanation of his reason for the complete re-examination of events and motive, Ron walked the Captain through each of the murders and attack with some degree of detail. He began with the murder of Terry Demming in the construction site as the first of the serial cases. He spent enough time on the details of the body's discovery to underline the lack of information about the cause of death, specifically the crushing of the head and neck that limited any chance of easily determining whether the death was caused by knife slash.

Captain Thorason accepted all this discussion without comment and only a few head nods.

Gene's contribution to the discussion was to provide what information was known about each victim. His recitation concerning Terry Demming was brief and consisted of the second-hand information he had obtained from Terry's mother in Las Vegas and what his co-worker, Bonnie, had to say about him. Ron and Gene agreed that a key piece of information involved Terry Demming applying to medical school, specifically to South West Ohio Medical School in Cincinnati.

Ron turned to his presentation of the murder of Dr. MacFarlane in his office at New City. He used two photographs of the crime scene to set the stage for his discussion of the killer's position to his victim at the point of the murder. He pointed out the blood spray that indicated the men were standing facing each other when the attack occurred. As the body was then found positioned in the desk chair, Ron proposed that the killer had helped his victim to be seated; examination of the desk chair did not reveal any fingerprints, leading Ron to conclude the killer wore gloves and that this was a premeditated murder.

Gene provided the composite picture they had of Dr. MacFarlane as a competent administrator but a personal 'teddy-bear', unlikely to knowingly provoke anger and always interested in avoiding a conflict. MacFarlane's job required that he convey unfortunate results of funding requests, and Gene provided quotes from the individuals who witnessed his announcement of funding loss to Adam Schlecter. The refrain of 'you're cutting my throat' was striking even as a stand-alone comment, but Gene amplified it by noting that Schlecter had said the same thing on losing his operating room privileges. He ended his part of the presentation by noting that Dr. MacFarlane had recently served three years of the medical school admissions committee and was known to advise prospective students about such a career.

Captain Thorason said, "Huh."

Ron talked about the murder scene involving Dr. Finkbeiner and showed the pertinent photographs. He noted how the blood splatter again best fit a scenario where the two individuals were facing each other and only an arm's length apart. The time of the death indicated that Finkbeiner was leaving the hospital. He had been accosted in the parking area as he prepared to get in his car. The separation of that attack and MacFarlane's murder by almost a week and the rampant discussion on the New City campus about Schlecter as the killer made Ron wonder why Finkbeiner would let him get so close.

Gene mentioned that the anesthesiologist had been involved with the operative case where the patient died from an operative error and for which Schlecter lost his privileges. He told of the review at New City, that found only a few other cases where the two worked together, and there had been no problems. Neither detective had to explain the meaning of that review to Thor. Gene told about their review of the files from the medical school. Finkbeiner had been a regular teacher in the physiology department. He also gave career advice to students in those classes, and interviewed and advised prospective students.

Captain Thorason leaned forward and placed his hands on his desk. "Huh," he said.

Ron sensed that they were losing the Captain's willingness to listen to minute detail, so he presented the murder scene involving Dr. Piringa quickly, emphasizing the closeness of the two persons in the murder and the site and time at the New City parking deck after regular hours. He quickly mentioned that the and Gene believed that the murderer was parked in the parking deck lying in wait for his victim. This had also allowed him to dodge the BOLO on his car.

Gene also jumped to his bottom line quickly. He noted that Piringa was a current member of the medical school admissions committee and a well-known advisor to prospective students. Captain Thorason did not bother with a comment; he immediately turned to Ron.

Ron then went over what they knew from the scene and interviews with Dr. Escobar. The attack followed almost exactly what happened with Finkbeiner and Piringa, the two involved persons standing an arm's length apart at the moment of attack. He noted that she could not identify her attacker other than as a White man.

Gene pointed out that Dr. Escobar was the current chair of the medical school admissions committee. Her medical specialty, pediatrics, made it unlikely she would have contact with Adam Schlecter.

Captain Thorason sniffed heavily, and they stopped their presentation, waiting for him to comment.

"Good," he said and nodded.

They took the nod as dismissal and left. Gene indicated that lunch was definitely needed before taking up the next step.

CHAPTER 50

Tuesday, April 12

Sandy was particularly busy serving other tables and booths that day, and they waited longer than usual to order. Ron decided he would change from a 'usual', which had become a cheeseburger and fries, to try the pastrami sandwich. Naturally, when he shared that information with Gene, it led to another discussion of intent.

"Why can't you just stick with the 'usual'? Are you trying to make some kind of statement here?"

"What are you thinking, bud? A statement about changing to a pastrami sandwich? What kind of statement do you think that is? Maybe I'm really Italian and have been hiding that for all these years?"

"It's not the pastrami, you know that. It's the change. Sandy may think you don't like the cheeseburger for some reason."

"It should be clear that I like the cheeseburger. I've ordered it six or eight times now."

"Then why change?"

"I like change, Gene. And it so happens that I like pastrami, too. There's this little sandwich shop in New Orleans, right off Canal Street that makes the absolute best hot pastrami sandwich I've ever had. And it would come with a wonderful pickle, too."

"Memories are great, but Sandy's memory of you right now is 'cheeseburger'."

"Really? You don't think the waitress can handle a change in my order from day to day?"

"Well, actually, I'm sure she can, but if you're not ordering a 'usual', she will have to stop and ask questions."

"Like what?"

"You know. What kind of mustard, what kind of bread, chips or fries. Everything."

"You're jealous."

Gene pulled himself up and frowned at his partner, "I am not."

"Sure you are. You don't want her to pay any more than the absolute minimum of time at our table talking to me and not you."

"That's not it at all. You're making that up."

"Am not."

"Are too."

Sandy appeared with two glasses of iced tea and asked, "Are you talking about Star Wars and that little droid?"

"What?" Gene asked, totally taken off guard.

"You know that little beeping thing called R-2."

Ron took up the conversation and got Sandy's attention. "No. We were actually arguing about the best items on the menu and I said I had not tried the pastrami yet."

"Oh," she said, smiling at him. "It's really good. The hot pastrami sandwich is my overall favorite."

"Well, that settles it for me," Ron smiled back. "Make that my order."

"Rye or whole wheat?"

"Rye, of course. Marble if you have it."

"Okay. Regular mustard or horseradish?"

"Definitely horseradish."

"Chips or fries?"

"Chips, please."

"Got it," she smiled at him and asked Gene, "The usual for you, honey?"

"Yes, thank you."

They silently watched her walk away from the table. Then Ron said, "See, no need for jealousy. You're still 'honey' in her book."

I'm not discussing this any further," Gene said, grinning as he picked up his tea.

"Well then, let's talk about this new list and the connection about the medical school admissions."

"I think that's a very clever idea you had," Gene said. But I don't see how it gets us any closer to Schlecter. And it certainly hasn't narrowed the potential field of additional victims."

"Yeah, I know. I think the idea was only partly helpful. We need to sit down quietly and review everything we have on the victims and see where the overlap is. It might not even be Schlecter."

"Now you're talking crazy talk. Why would that happen?"

"Well, it still could be we can't find him because he went off on sabbatical and has nothing to do with this string of attacks."

"I don't believe that."

"I know, Gene. But we have to consider it. Did you bring the list?"

"Don't need it. Got all the pertinent info right here," he said, tapping his forehead.

"Great. We don't have to go back to the office. Let's just run the facts on everybody again.

They were interrupted a few minutes later as Sandy brought them their food. There was no attempt to continue working once the food arrived, either. Each man turned to their respective sandwich and began eating, mostly in silence. Soon, however, Ron's "M'mmm" seemed to accompany every bite of the pastrami sandwich.

Gene finally recognized the implication with, "I presume your sounds of satisfaction indicate a degree of happiness with your order?"

Ron spoke around a partially full mouth, "You betcha. This is superb. Warm pastrami with horseradish mustard on marble rye." He swallowed and took a deep drink of tea. "I should have been ordering this all along. And so should you."

"Maybe. You are making it sound like a perfect lunch. I shall perhaps try it in the future."

"Now, don't go jumping the fence on that 'usual' thing. Maybe try it just once."

"Huh."

"Yeah, right. Now, what do we know that might tie all these people together."

Gene finished his patty melt and pushed the plate aside. "I think there's one thing in the list has makes me wonder about it."

"Okay. What's that?"

"From the involvement of the chair of the Admissions Committee at the medical school to the people at New City, all of them were on one side of the table."

"Meaning?"

"Meaning that everyone on our list was a decision-maker. Their recommendation could make or break a prospective medical student. For some of them, their support could directly influence who got in and who didn't."

"Right. And some are currently in that position and others were in that position in the recent past. Even those who are only interviewers."

"My point exactly. All of them, except one."

"Well, I guess that's so."

"Terry Demming was not a decision-maker in the admissions process. He was a pawn. He was waiting for a decision. So why is he on the list?"

"That is strange. What do we know about him?"

"Really just some bits and pieces. He graduated from UNLV but came to Ohio to apply to medical school. That seems odd."

Ron noted, "Tom told me once that lots of kids try that because Ohio has so many schools. If they can establish a residence here, and that only takes a year, then they can apply as a resident."

"Still, coming here to establish residence suggests he didn't get in at home."

"Yes, it does. Do we know that?"

"Not for sure. Remember when we looked at his crib we found that pay stub from a hospital in Akron. So, it looks like he's been in the state shopping around."

"That Bonnie person told me he was applying to South West medical School here and hoping to get a strong recommendation from Schlecter."

"Well, that didn't go so well for him."

Ron pushed his plate away and said, "Pretty clear to me, partner. We need more information on this guy to match with the others. Let's get back to the office and do some deep drilling."

"I was planning on having some pie."

"Get it to go. I'll have the car out front in five."

CHAPTER 51

Tuesday, April 12

They spent the rest of the afternoon chasing leads at some distance over the telephone. Gene called UNLV and contacted the registrar's office. He spoke with a young lady who was pleasant and knowledgeable but who had no intention of 'violating privacy' by revealing Terry Demming's personal information, his coursework, or his grades. She was so concerned about Gene's request that he finally had to ask to speak to her supervisor. That person happened to not be in the office at the moment. The young woman was about to terminate the conversation when Gene asked to speak to the registrar. He found himself put on hold without music.

He cradled the phone on his shoulder and took a bite of his pie. Ron noticed this and asked, "They put you on hold, didn't they?"

Gene just nodded and took another bite. The pie was quite tasty, but he wished he had insisted on getting a cup of coffee to go with it. He was about to say something to Ron when a deep and resonant voice came over the line, "This is Dr. Robbins. May I help you?"

"Sir, my name is Gene Novalchek. I am a detective in the homicide division of the Cincinnati Police Department."

"I see. And you want information on a student?"

"Yes, sir. The student was there a few years ago. His name is Terry Demming. I believe the young lady I spoke with had already pulled his record."

"She did, and I have it in front of me."

"This young man is a person of interest in a murder investigation. In fact, he is the one who was murdered. We are trying to determine connections between him and others in the case."

"Oh, my goodness. You say he was murdered?"

"Yes. And there were some other murders, as well. We are trying to make connections to see if there is a common link between the cases."

"What was your name again?"

"Novalchek. Gene Novalchek. A detective with the Cincinnati Homicide Division."

"And your badge number?"

Gene hesitated for a second. Then he gave his badge number and asked, "What would you need that for?"

"I'll call you right back, detective," came the sonorous answer. The line went dead.

Gene hung up, looked at Ron, shrugged, and took another bite of pie.

Three minutes later, the phone on Gene's desk rang. He picked it up and answered, "Novalchek."

"Detective, this is Dr. Robbins. I will be happy to share this information with you.

"Great. We know his home address, and I have already spoken with his mother. What we would like is any other information you can provide to help us talk to people who knew him while he was there at the university."

"I have an address that appears to be a duplex in the student housing."

"That would be helpful."

"It appears that Mr. Demming was a pre-medicine student, but … Hmm. It also appears that his grades in the obligatory courses were not strong."

"Meaning?"

"Well, I would imagine he had some difficulty in gaining admission to medical school with these grades."

"I think you are right about that. We have no information to indicate that he ever got in. He was likely here in Ohio for that purpose, though. Can you recommend an instructor for us to contact?"

Gene got the name and telephone number of the pre-med advisor listed on Terry's record. He thanked Mr. Robbins and hung up. He quickly finished the remainder of his pie and looked over at Ron, who was engaged in a deep conversation on the phone himself. After stretching his neck to relieve the tightness caused by the prolonged cradling of the phone, he sighed, and lifted the receiver, and dialed the cell phone number of Terry's advisor at UNLV.

Ron, meanwhile, had telephoned the Human Resources department at Akron General Hospital. The pay stub gave him a period of time and an employee number. He was able to find a Personnelist agreeable to provide information. The information, itself, however, was limited and not particularly illuminating. Terry apparently had worked at the hospital for only a few months as a phlebotomist. The Personnelist said the record was virtually empty. The only other information was a local address. Ron thanked the man and wrote down what he could.

Ron noted that Gene was having a spirited conversation with someone who seemed to be arguing about releasing information. He turned on his computer and went to a government site where police could cross an address with telephone numbers. He chose the Akron directory and plugged in the address he got from the Personnelist. In just a few minutes, he was able to find the address and an associated telephone number. He looked up at Gene and realized he was no longer on the phone and was about to say something to his partner when Gene's phone rang, and he answered. Ron picked up his own desk phone and called the address in Akron. Someone answered on the third ring.

"Yup."

Since he did not have a name to match with the address, Ron asked if he had the right telephone number and address.

"Yup."

"This is Detective Ron Looney of the Cincinnati Homicide Division. I'm looking for information about Terry Demming."

"He doesn't live here anymore."

"Actually, I was aware of that. To whom am I speaking?"

"Bill… Billy."

"And your last name, Bill?"

"Whitman. Like the candy."

"Mr. Whitman, we are aware that Mr. Demming left Akron to come to Cincinnati. We are seeking more information about his reason for that move."

"Is Terry okay? I mean, you said 'homicide', right?"

"Mr. Whitman, I'm sorry to say that we believe Terry Demming was the victim of a serial killer. We are trying to get information about him that might help us to locate his killer."

"Wow! Serial killer. And all he ever wanted was to go to medical school."

"Do you know why he left Akron? I mean, you've got a medical school right there. Wasn't he trying to get in there?"

"Yeah, I'm pretty sure he was. We talked about that a little. But he said that he talked to some advisor there at Northeast who told him he was never going to get into medical school with his undergraduate grades. So, Terry spent about three days looking for a graduate program where he could go get a Master's degree that would help him get in."

"And that's why he came to Cincinnati?"

"Well, I know he looked in Cleveland and Columbus and Cincinnati for what he called "the right program". Then one day he was gone. I thought he must have found that program. But he never told me what he found or where he was going."

"What was the last day you know he was in Akron?"

It took Bill Whitman some time to determine when he last saw Terry. His memory included checking a wall calendar for party dates, trying to remember whether he brought anyone home from the party and whether Terry was there when he did. He finally settled on a date that was a few months before Terry showed up on the payroll at New City.

As Ron looked up, he noted that Gene had gotten off the phone and was rubbing his eyes. Ron thanked Bill Whitman and disengaged his call without promising to let Mr. Whitman know whatever happened to his former roommate.

Gene asked, "Anything I need to hear before I go take a shower?"

"Not really. I know he left Akron because he wasn't going to get in the medical school there."

"And I know his college grades weren't going to get that job done anywhere."

"I still don't have a handle on this guy, though. What was he doing here in Cincinnati for months before he showed up in Schlecter's lab?'

"Can we think more about that tomorrow?"

"Sure. I'd prefer a nice peaceful night, too."

Chapter 52

Wednesday, April 13

Ron walked into the Dick Pen at eight-fifteen the next morning. He didn't pay much attention to Gene's empty desk because he knew his partner would not likely be in all day.

Gene had called Ron around six that morning. "Hey, partner, I got a situation here at the house and gotta take a personal day."

Ron was not quite awake and still managed to ask, "What's up?"

"We've got a broken water line in the unit right above me, and I'm already standing in water above my shoes. The landlord's here, and we're trying to find the valve. But this place is a mess, and I'm gonna be awhile getting it straight."

"Yeah. Yeah. Sorry, man. You need a place to sleep or anything?"

"I don't know yet. This is a real can of worms."

"Well, don't worry about the case. Remember, all we were gonna do was make calls. I'll take care of it."

"Just don't go make some giant breakthrough complete with arrests, and all I get to see is the story in the newspapers.

"Yeah. Don't worry. I'll hold plenty of paperwork back for you to do."

"Thanks, man, Tell Thor, okay?"

"Sure."

Ron actually remembered the conversation when his alarm went off thirty minutes later. He told Meg that Gene might have to come live with them as he went in the shower. She didn't respond.

Knowing he was going it alone for the day, Ron picked up some breakfast burritos and coffee on his way to the office. After putting his packages on his desk, he stuck his head in Captain Thorason's office to let him know about Gene's absence. The captain looked up and said, "Huh."

Looney had skipped breakfast at home to get an earlier start on his calls. But, after going by the burrito joint and the coffee shop, he found he was starting at about the same time anyway. Wondering what had ever possessed him willingly to trade Meg's breakfast for a commercial one, he ate the first burrito while laying out his notepad and the list of needed calls.

He made the first call back to Akron General. He had the name and shift for Terry Demming's supervisor in the phlebotomy unit. He found her in her office.

"Phlebotomy. How can I help?" she asked on answering.

"Is this Laura Longstreth?"

"Yes, it is."

"Ms. Longstreth, my name is Ron Loony. I am a detective in the homicide division of the Cincinnati police department."

"Oh, my. Yes. How can I help you?"

"Do you recall a man who worked for you a couple of years ago named Terry Demming?"

"Uh, yes. Yes, I do. Not here very long. Why?"

Ignoring her question, Ron went on, "What can you tell me about him?"

She was silent for a moment and then, "As I recall, he was a good worker. Always on time and willing to take some overtime. Why do you want to know?"

"Do you know why he left?"

"I remember a couple of the others saying he was trying to get into medical school and was turned down here at Northeast Ohio. Did you say homicide? Is he all right?"

"Ms. Longstreth, we are investigating a series of murders here in Cincinnati and trying to make connections between the victims, and …"

"Victims? Was Terry a victim?"

Ron paused for a moment and then said, "We think he was one of the victims, yes, and we would like to know more about him so we can …"

She interrupted again, "He said he had finally gotten to a good place."

"What's that?"

"Terry told me that he had finally gotten to a good place."

"When did he say this?" Ron was enthused about finding someone who had a personal connection to Terry.

"I got a postcard from him a few weeks after he left us. He said he was enrolled in a Master's program at Cincinnati State in medical informatics and was applying to Southwest for medical school."

"That is very helpful information, Ms. Longstreth."

"And now he's dead?"

"Yes, ma'am. I'm sorry."

"That's just tragic. He was such a good kid. Friendly, solid worker. Really good with the kids."

"Kids?"

"We put him on pediatrics because he could always get the kids to go along with him drawing their blood."

"Is there anything else you can tell me about him?"

"Not at the moment."

Ron gave her his name and telephone number in case she remembered anything else and hung up. He looked at the telephone and wondered about the relationship between the young man and the older woman boss. The information from Gene's call suggested an apparent distance between Terry and his mother. Apparently, Terry had a closer relationship with Laura Longstreth.

Looney sat back in his chair and took a long swig on his coffee. He grabbed the other burrito and unwrapped it quickly, intending to eat it before his coffee cooled. The burrito only required four bites before it was gone. A minute later, the coffee was, too. Ron wished that Gene were present to discuss the recent call, but he wasn't. He turned back to his list and added an annotation to call the Cincinnati State Medical Informatics program.

He was able to find correct numbers in the telephone directory to connect with the program office on campus. The young man who answered the phone, however, brought Ron's progress to a halt. He knew nothing about previous students or how to find out anything about them. After a few minutes, Ron guessed this young man was new in the job and asked, "Can I speak to the program director?"

That request also seemed to be above the young man's pay grade. Without explanation, he found himself put on hold. A few minutes later, an older woman came on the line and asked, soothingly, "Can I help you?"

"Yes, ma'am. My name is detective Ron Looney with the Cincinnati Police Department. I would like some information about one of your previous students." Ron decided to leave the fact he was from homicide out of the discussion since it tended to cause questions.

"And who would that be, detective?"

"Terry Demmings. He enrolled maybe a year ago."

"Let me see."

Everything became quiet at the other end for a short while, and then Ron thought he could hear computer keyboard sounds. She came back on asking, "One 'M' or two?"

"Ah, two 'M's'. Demming," he spelled.

"Uh-huh. Yes, he's right here. And what did you want to know?"

"Did he have an advisor or counselor for this degree?"

"Oh, yes. Every one of our masters' students has an academic advisor. His was Gerry Crump."

"And how can I reach Mr. Crump?"

"I can give you *Doctor* Crump's office phone."

"Thank you, ma'am," Ron said, reddening slightly and glad no one could see it.

Doctor Crump did not answer the number he had been given, so Ron decided to get another coffee and think things over. He checked with the Captain, who indicated a cup of coffee would suit him just fine. As he walked down the stairs and further down the block to the coffee shop he thought about Terry Demming. He was beginning to get a picture of this striving young man and again, wished he had his partner to discuss his findings with.

He brought the coffees back, shared a brief moment with the Captain, noted that he had not heard back from Gene, and returned to his desk. This time, his call to the Cincinnati State campus was answered.

"Crump."

"Dr. Crump, my name is Ron Looney. I am a detective with the Cincinnati Police Department. I'd like to talk to you about one of the students you advised a year or so ago, Terry Demming."

"Okay. I remember Terry. Average guy, I guess."

"Can you tell me anything about why he left your program?"

"I can tell you exactly what he told me."

"All right. Please."

"He said he was getting the masters to help with his application to medical school."

"Yes, we knew that."

"Then, one day, I walk in the lab, and he is packing all his stuff up."

"You mean to leave?"

"Yes. And when I asked him about it, he said his advisor at Southwest said this degree would not help him with admission. Hah!"

"Do you disagree?"

"I don't know anything about their admissions process or expectations at the medical school, but if he was taking up a seat and intended not to practice what we teach, then we are all better off with him gone."

"I see."

"The medical profession is going to need more of us than doctors very soon!"

"Do you know who that advisor was?"

 "No. No one from around here, I can tell you that."

"Thank you, Dr. Crump."

Looney hung up and rubbed his eyes. 'Who could that advisor be?' he wondered. It had to be someone at the medical school. Probably. Maybe. The school has 'advisors' all over. He thought, 'I should call Gene.'

CHAPTER 53

Wednesday, April 13

L ooney didn't call Gene. At least not right then. Rocky and Harry were noisily getting together to go to lunch and saw him sitting by himself. That wouldn't do in their opinion. Rocky hollered at him across the Pen, "Hey, Walker. Lunch with your friends?"

Ron looked up and waved, initially thinking he would get something to go and take it to Gene's. The friendly waving from the two changed his mind, however. He grinned and nodded, got up, grabbed his coat, and headed out the door with them.

They went to a burger joint close to the Stadium. Apparently, they were well known in this place, as he and Gene were at the café where Sandy worked. The clientele was somewhat more blue-collar than where he usually ate. The waitresses were older and more matronly, and the menu did not list either pastrami or key lime pie. But it did have an offering of a 'big' Reuben sandwich, and Ron made that his choice.

Rocky and Harry had their own cases and made a few coded references to things they needed to get done after lunch while Ron decided on his order. Once everyone had made their choice and gotten their drinks, Rocky turned to Ron and asked, "Okay, Walker, tell us what's up with the serial killer business. You about to close it?"

"You know how it is," Looney replied. "Just plodding along and grabbing at straws."

"We heard Gene was looking to start some college courses," Harry grinned.

"Yeah, he's been calling all over the country but can't find one that'll let him in," Rocky added. "That's what we heard."

"You've been feeding doughnuts to Sallie at the switchboard to get that information," Ron jibed back.

"And now he's taking off from work," Harry went on.

Well, he wouldn't have wanted to get his suit dirty coming to lunch with us," Rocky added. "Not like our ole buddy, Walker."

"You know, I can tell you're setting me up for something here, right?" Ron said, lifting his glass.

"Well, what if we are? This is all between friends, right?"

"Depends. Are you buying my lunch or what?"

"Hey, we're not that serious."

"Hmmm."

"I mean, Harry and I were talking about things, you know, and thinking that maybe you and Gene could use a little help running down some leads and things like that. Eh?"

Ron looked at Rocky over his glass and said, "You must think we're just about to pop this one if you think you can jump in at this late date and get credit for the solve."

Rocky tried to look contrite but couldn't pull it off. He began laughing and elbowed Harry, "I told you Walker was too smart for us."

Ron changed the subject, "What was that you were saying about needing to get a warrant when you get back to the office?"

"Yeah, we're working that murder downtown, and we think the guy had been in one of the backroom gambling sites before he was taken out and whacked."

"Which one?"

"Out near Findley."

"What did you want from me?"

Both of the other men paid attention to their drinks until Rocky said, "We remember you patrolled that area."

"C'mon, fellas. That was a decade ago."

"But you probably still got some 'friends' out there, right?"

"Listen, any friends I had in OTR back then are now dead or in jail."

They stared at him until he continued, "Look, I left OTR over eight years ago. And I only had two guys there who would give me tips. Both of them are dead. Anybody else I know from there has been in jail for years. I got no touch on those streets. Sorry."

"Well, it was worth a try."

"Still gonna buy my lunch?"

"Hell, no. You didn't give anything up."

After lunch, driving back to the office in Harry's car, Looney noticed more than a little heartburn. His Reuben had been satisfyingly greasy and wonderfully spicy, but he was paying the piper for enjoying it so much.

"You got any Maalox?" he asked Harry.

"Not in the car. Got some in my desk."

"What's the matter, Walker?" Rocky wanted to know. "Eating with your buddies disagree with you?"

"It may be my buddies, but I really think it was the Reuben."

He got a couple of Maalox tablets from Harry and chewed them up immediately on returning to his desk. He had a cache of small bottles of water in his lower drawer and got one of them to sip on until his stomach calmed down. Sitting there and waiting for coolness to return to his abdomen, Looney decided he should call Gene.

Gene's answered his cell phone before the second ring. "Hey, I was thinking I might call and see what's going on."

"Well, the biggest thing is I had lunch with Rocky and Harry at some greasy spoon and now have heartburn."

"Sandy would have been happy to see you."

"I'm sure, but I was actually gonna grab something and come to your house. Then Rocky invited me, and … well, I went."

"Not to worry. I got some pizza for us guys here."

"Big crowd?"

"Not really. The plumber came and tore some holes in the wall and ceiling to get to the broken pipe. He left an hour ago. I got some guys in here now assessing the damage and deciding how much more wall or ceiling needs replacement."

"Insurance?"

"Yep. That guy comes this weekend to look at the damage. We can't really fix anything until then. But, it's not raining inside my apartment anymore. You got something?"

"Ah, not really. I've been on the phone filling in some detail about our boy Terry."

"Helpful."

"Not so much. Pretty much the expected. Good kid, Hard worker, wanted to go to medical school."

"No other connections, huh?"

"Nope. I'm gonna go back out to New City to check his application there."

"Why? Did we miss something?"

"I don't know, Gene. All we got was addresses. Maybe there's more. I don't know."

"All right. Tell Nick he owes me one."

Ron didn't give Nick that message. The cluster of people at the kiosk in the New City lobby kept him from any conversation with the barista. Looney got his 'usual' and found his way down to the HR office. He told the clerk at the front desk what he wanted and soon spoke to the same Personnelist that helped them before. Once again, he received the paper folder and instructions not to leave the area with it. He thumbed quickly through the few pages in Terry Demming's personnel folder and noted the addresses that Gene had written down before. He was about to give the folder back when he noticed writing on the back of one of the sheets.

Looney turned over the sheet and noted a short handwritten note in a blank area that asked for an applicant to tell why he was applying for this particular position. In small, careful handwriting, presumably belonging to Terry Demming, he read of his long-standing interest in medicine, his great desire for a career in medicine, and his belief that having a responsible technical position in Adam Schlecter's laboratory would help him gain admission to Southwest Ohio Medical School.

The applicant ended his statement by noting that he had confidence in his own ability to succeed and believed the position he was seeking would help him reach his goal because he had been told so by his primary advisor, the chairman of the research committee: Dr. Donald Piringa.

On his way home from New City, Ron called the morgue and asked to speak to Dr. Darringer.

"Darringer."

"Hey doc, it's Walker. Any info on that construction site body?"

"No. I told you, detective, we have several other cases in front of that one. You have an I.D. The cause of death is going to be very difficult because of the injuries to the head."

There was a brief silence, and then she went on, "What is it. Walker? Really, what is going on? What do you need? You've got good instincts. Why are you pushing me on this?"

"I don't know, doc. I kinda think there's something there we oughta know. Gut thinking, that's all."

"I'll see if I can do something soon," she promised and hung up.

Looney headed home thinking about a cold beer and some quiet reflection on the patio.

CHAPTER 54

Friday, April 15

The news that the body found at the construction site was not Terry Demming, but Adam Schlecter spread quickly. Ron called Tom Bolling to let him know as soon as he hung up the phone with Darringer. He also went immediately back into Captain Thorason's office to update him on the change in thought. He already had a plan to deal with the new information.

Tom played his inside knowledge for all it was worth, waiting to reveal it at the morning meeting. He waited until Sam had reviewed the G and L sheet and determined there were no other major issues for discussion. Then he announced, "Detective Looney called me to say they have found Adam Schlecter."

Everyone in the room, especially the nurses, took deep breaths and smiled tersely.

"Where was he?" Sam asked reasonably.

"Turns out he was hiding sorta in plain sight."

"Where?" asked Roslyn.

"In the dirt, actually. At the scene of the first murder. He was the victim. He's been dead all along."

There were several gasps and shakes of the head and murmurs of concern as Tom made eye contact with everyone at the table.

"Well," Roslyn announced, "I'm certainly glad we have cleared that up. We certainly don't want people thinking our physicians are murderers."

"Huh," Tom said, staring at her.

Alena Preston nodded vigorously in agreement with her boss and turned her attention to meticulously straightening the papers in front of her.

Tom looked at Mastone, who was staring back at him.

"What do you think, Sam? Everything all cleared up."

"Yes. Yes, I think so. Are they still looking for whoever did these murders?"

"Good change of pace, Sam. Yes, Detective Looney tells me their primary interest now is trying to find Terry Demming."

Looney and Gene began reworking their list of connections to account for Terry as the potential killer. Ron was struck by how quickly things started to come together with this new perspective. They continued to speculate about a 'trigger event', and Ron decided to ask Tom. A quick phone call was all that was needed.

"Bolling"

"Hey, General."

"Oh boy. Here we go again. First, you call and drop a bomb about finding Schlecter's body, and now you want some favor from me."

"Why do you say that? I didn't ask for anything."

"Because you never call me, 'General' unless you want a favor of some kind."

"That's not true."

"Ron, don't you try to pull something on another Razorback. I've been watching you pull this 'General' stuff for years now. What do you want?"

"We're trying to figure out what started all this killing. It seems most likely that this Demming kid went off the rails right about the same time Schlecter lost his research money. Do you think that could have done it?"

"I don't know, Ron. It doesn't make the most sense. What are you thinking is the connection Terry has to any other the other deaths?"

"Looks to us like everybody was involved in some way with medical school admissions. We know he was trying to get in. That's about it."

"When do you think the killings started? The one in the construction, I mean. You know, Schlecter."

"Well, we think he probably did plan to take off for some kind of sabbatical around the middle of March. MacFarlane gave him the bad news on the fifteenth, and nobody saw him or Demming after that."

"Fifteenth? Let me make a call. Or, maybe you would like to make this one yourself."

"This is Doctor Escobar. Can I help you?"

"Good day, doctor. This is Detective Looney."

"Ah, yes. Detective. Do you need something?"

"Yes, actually I do. Can you tell me about individuals that applied to medical school but were turned down?"

"I can tell you there were many."

"How does your process work?"

"First, detective, this is a committee decision, not mine alone. I lead the committee to make consensus decisions.

"How do you do that?"

"We get more than four hundred applications for the hundred-twenty seats in our school each year. The admissions office is responsible for handling every application. Each applicant's information is collected into a single folder that is kept in the admissions office.

We start collecting the information in August, and some folders are available for review by committee members starting in mid-September."

"This goes on for a long time, then."

"Oh yes. We have fifteen members on the committee, some from the school, some from private practice, and some from the business community. Each member is expected to physically come to the Office to review and score every application. The committee meets as a body of the whole every week beginning in mid-December. The agenda at each meeting includes a discussion of each applicant screened by at least twelve committee members. We actually call the record complete when at least twelve members have reviewed the folder."

"And then what, you vote?"

"Essentially, yes. We discuss and agree to a breakpoint in the list of screened applicants. Above the breakpoint, everyone agrees all applicants should be offered a seat. The staff sends them an acceptance letter and track who accepts. Part of the agenda each week involves learning about acceptances and how many seats remain vacant.

"Some turn down the offer?"

"Yes, of course. These students are applying to several schools, and they take the best offer they have. The early choices are the best students, and every school wants them. So, we may only get acceptance letters from thirty to forty percent of the ones we write."

"When is this all over?"

"We keep going down our list, accepting the best candidates until all our seats are full."

"When is that?"

"Well, we never say we are finished until March fifteen. That's the national day for final letters of acceptance."

"What do you do with those you don't accept?"

"Well, we write them a note. The Dean usually tries to soften the blow with some words about the difficulty in making decisions involving so many candidates and so few seats."

"When would the last person denied a seat be notified of that decision?"

"March fifteenth."

"Can you tell me if Terry Demming was on the last list for denial?"

"Yes, of course, I can. This year our discussion came down to five people for the last two seats. Mr. Demming was one of those. Two other applicants were chosen, so I know he would have gotten the denial letter. On March fifteen."

"Pretty good memory, Dr. Or are you referring to notes?"

"No, I have reason to remember Terry Demming. I had interviewed him for admission."

Chapter 55

Friday, April 15

The meeting in Captain Thorason's office was subdued but charged with some electricity by the feeling that the investigation had made significant progress. The Captain was once again mostly monosyllabic in his contributions, and Ron and Gene sometimes talked over each other in their attempt to give him the good news.

Ron took advantage of the opportunity to re-cast the story from a new perspective. He used the information he and Gene had collected to depict Terry Demming as an intense, goal-driven young man with average grades who desperately wanted to be admitted to medical school. He had been rejected by his home state of Arizona and near-by states and had taken some widely-known information to come to Ohio to seek entrance to the profession. Ohio provided the opportunity for students to apply to its multiple schools as residents of the state. The state requirement to establishing residency only required one year of living in-state.

Terry Demming started his Ohio experience in Akron working in a major hospital associated with a medical school. Sources at North East Ohio Medical University, or NEOMED, informed him that his poor undergraduate grades were a major impediment to his acceptance. Someone suggested he attain a Master's degree to become a successful candidate. A former roommate supplied information that Terry enrolled in a degree program at Cincinnati State in Medical Informatics, left Akron, and moved to Cincinnati. Once he arrived, he began making contact with the South West Ohio Medical School. He contacted the school and was interviewed by Dr. Escobar. Somehow he made contact with Dr. Piringa, who agreed to advise him on his quest. Piringa had recommended he get a job in research. Terry mentioned this in his application. Piringa apparently specifically recommended Adam Schlecter's work. Terry also dropped out of the degree program because someone, at this point unknown, had told him a degree in medical informatics would not be impressive to any medical school admissions committee.

Bonnie Phillips said Terry believed that the work he was doing in Schlecter's laboratory would get him into medical school. Bonnie thought she remembered Terry saying he met an anesthesiologist at the gym. This physician ostensibly told Terry to look for a job at New City. Ron guessed that might have led Terry to Dr. Piringa. Bonnie agreed the work in Schlecter's laboratory would certainly have made a significant impact on disease treatment. Any notoriety from the laboratory's success would probably have improved Terry's chances of medical school admission. As Ron put the story together, Terry's letter of rejection from SWOMS arrived probably the same day Schlecter was notified he lost his funding.

"Huh," Said the Captain.

"That's right," Ron replied. "Had to be the worst set of circumstances piled on each other at that moment. Bonnie said she never saw either of them again."

Gene added, "The evidence we gathered from Schlecter's home right after the MacFarlane murder was most consistent with him packing to leave. His suitcase was gone, clothes were gone, and hangers were bare. We thought he was running."

"Huh"

"Yes, we all did," Ron added. "For some reason, it appears that Schlecter went back to the laboratory after packing his car. He must have changed into scrubs and done something in the laboratory, but when he left, he was car-jacked by Terry."

"Terry drove him to the construction site and killed him. Terry thought he lost his chance to get in medical school with the loss of Schlecter's funding. I don't know. But clearly, he blamed Schlecter for some part in his own failure."

Gene noted, "We don't really know if Terry had put his own car there earlier or if he brought it back later. But he found Schlecter's car to have multiple changes of clothes, cash, and the parking deck automated entry card. So he took it and left his along with his identification."

Ron picked up the thread by revisiting the MacFarlane murder. He pointed out that, at the time, this was the only murder they were aware of, and the search for motive did not mention anything related to Demming. The result was to start the search for Adam Schlecter, known to have argued with the deceased.

"Huh."

"Absolutely. And the second murder just made that seem even more correct. The death of the anesthesia guy from an operation that ended up causing Schlecter to lose his operating privileges just fit in with the picture of an angry guy out to avenge himself."

"Hmm."

"Actually, no, we don't know exactly how Dr. Finkbeiner fits in to the Terry Demming scenario. He was known to interview prospective medical students, so they may have come in contact somehow. That's a little murky right now, sir. I think he was the guy that Terry met at the gym that got him interested in New City in the first place. But we may never know."

"Huh."

"Moving on, we believe that Terry used the key card and Schlecter's Mercedes to hide from surveillance in the hospital parking deck. That also allowed him to watch for others he wanted to take revenge on, like Piringa and Finkbeiner. And stay out of our sight."

Gene emphasized, "There's always some cars in the parking deck around the clock, so nobody would find it strange. He may even have moved the car every day to minimize suspicion. We don't have proof of this because the parking deck card reader doesn't have a system to log in users. It just responds to the card signal."

The Captain nodded.

"But, he had to come out to get to Dr. Escobar. He probably went after her on foot."

Gene broke in to say, "Odd thing, there. She completely blocked his knife thrust and even knocked the knife out of his hand because she is left-handed. The other victims were all right-handed.

Ron added, "Plus, she plays squash and has a wicked forehand." He looked at the Captain's raised eyebrows for a second and then added, "At least, that's what she says."

"Huh."

"So, now we have a much clearer picture of the murders. I mean, motive and means, at least. And we are circulating a picture of Terry with a new BOLO. Still looking for the Mercedes, of course." Ron was wrapping up.

Gene spoke before the Captain could respond, "We certainly don't believe that he is finished with his spree. We continue to be concerned about another attack on Dr. Escobar, and we have her under watch."

Ron added as they both rose and moved toward the door, "We're going to go back over all the interviews, too. There may be someone else he wants to kill."

"Huh." This came with a smile and a nod.

Chapter 56

Friday, April 15

They both agreed that a session like that required another cup of coffee. They put their papers on their desks and scooted down the back stairs. As they walked toward the coffee shop, they tended to jostle each other at the shoulder and grin like teenagers.

The presentation had also made them hungry, so they each got a pastry, Ron the morning bun, and Gene a crème filled Danish. With coffee in hand, they found their favorite small table in the back corner. Each of them could have their back to a wall and could visualize the rest of the shop and the front door. No surprises.

Such positioning had long been Ron's habit, and he converted Gene to his way of thinking early in their career together. His explanation was initially historical.

"Historical?" Gene asked. "What kind of history?"

"American. Police work."

"Tell me, please."

"Wild Bill Hickok was shot in the back because he sat with his back to the door."

"You made that up."

"History, my good man. History. Truth from the Old West. Shot in the back by Broken Nose Jack McCall in Deadwood, South Dakota. You can look it up."

"Oh, trust me. I will"

Gene had found the story to be absolutely true and asked if that was the only reason Ron always took the seat facing the doorway.

"Nope. Just good sense to be able to see trouble coming" was the answer he got. The more he thought about it, the more sense it made, especially for a pair of cops. So he began to want to have his back covered, too. Ron understood the impulse, and they decided to seek out seating arrangements where each of them could have their 'back to the wall', as it were. Their coffee shop table was one of their favorites.

"That went well," Gene started. "Not nearly as much talking out of him."

"Yeah, I think he was pleased to see the break-through. I bet he's calling upstairs, right now."

They each took a moment to savor a bite of pastry and a sip of hot coffee.

"I knew a guy in the service who would relish times like these," Ron noted.

"What part? Updating the boss? Having our backs covered?"

"The time when it was appropriate to stop for a second and enjoy the fruits of one's labors."

"That's us, I guess."

"He used to say to me at the end of a shift, "Hey, it's time for sweet bread and hot coffee."

"I like that. Sweet bread and hot coffee. I suggest we make that our motto."

"Gene, we don't need a motto that suggests eating. You do that well enough."

"All right, then. Here's to more times to relish." They saluted each other with their cups.

"Except we need to apprehend this Terry guy," Ron noted. "Job isn't over 'til then."

Gene nodded soberly, wiped the last crumbs from his lips, and said, "Where are we gonna start?"

"First, we need to be certain he's still hanging around and not run off."

"Why would he run?"

Several reasons I can think of. First, he may be done. He may have already attacked and killed everyone on his death list."

Gene held up his hand. "Well, he wasn't successful with Escobar. If you think he won't leave until his work is done, what about her? That would make me think he's gonna make another run at her."

Ron nodded. "I was saying he may have intended to *try* to kill everyone on his list. It could be that his failure with Escobar brings everything to an end. But you're right; he could still want another shot at her. We've got sufficient coverage on her, however, and it's not hidden. He'd be nuts to attempt something with the uniforms standing by."

"I think he is nuts, for the record. But maybe not suicidal nuts."

"My concern is he may have other people on his list, and we don't have any idea who they may be."

"Bonnie didn't have any other names, did she?"

"Nope. And the only thing we know that ties everyone together on this mythical list is medical school admission activity. And there are plenty of others with that same characteristic."

"Do you think the Dean might have another way to get names?" Gene was clearly reaching and grabbing at straws, but his question did make Ron sit up more straight and cock his head.

"I'm calling," he said, pulling out his cell phone and starting to dial.

Gene leaned back with a small sense of satisfaction that his idea brought such quick action. Shirley, the Dean's secretary, answered.

"May I speak to Dean Wisener, please?" Ron said.

Gene watched as his partner began to clench and unclench the fist of his free hand.

"Okay, Thank you, Shirley. Two things then, One, do you know if she ever counseled a student named Terry Demming, and Two exactly where did she go?" Ron looked up at Gene wide-eyed and made a face. He listened another few seconds and then repeated, "How about the interview with Terry Demming?.. Yes, I'll wait."

He covered the phone and said to Gene, "She's gone off to the ballgame. Her husband is a season ticket holder."

"Reds?"

"Yes, they go early and eat at the stadium."

"Huh."

"Doesn't have the same cachet as it does when Thor says that."

"I know. I was just thinking …"

He was interrupted by Ron turning back to the phone. "Yes, right here… I appreciate that, Shirley. Thank you so much."

"What's the deal?" Gene wanted to know.

"Dean Wisener met with a Terry Demming back last year for 'career counseling'. Something about how best to get into medical school."

"You think he's after her?"

"I'd bet on it, and he's likely gonna do it at the ballpark because he can cause a stir and get away. We gotta go."

They chugged the end of their coffee and headed for the car. On the way, Gene reasonably asked, "Did you get the seat number where she'll be?"

"Shirley didn't know that. But she did know what section. It's in the club."

Chapter 57

Friday, April 15

"There's a club at the ballpark?"

"C'mon, Gene, you know there is, Every park has a club for the high rollers. The GA isn't any different."

"Yeah, I know. I wish I had the money to join the club at the ballpark."

"Really, I didn't know you would be interested in that."

"Oh, I'm not. I just wish I had the money. That's not what I would do with it, I just wish I had it."

"Get in, Gene."

Taking Ron's car they pulled out of the garage and headed west on Ezzard Charles. Gene was still fumbling with his seat belt as Ron passed the Catholic School.

"Have you shortened these belts?"

"I have not. Perhaps our lunches are growing on you."

"I resemble that remark. Look out! "

"Don't yell, Gene. I saw that guy and he saw me."

"Why don't you use the light?"

"Good idea," Ron showed his agreement by turning on the flasher and lightly touching the siren. Cars dutifully pulled to the side to allow them to pass. Moments later they screeched their wheels turning left onto Western Avenue and then immediately onto the I-75 south.

Neither of them spoke for a couple of minutes. The flashers and the siren helped clear a way through the going home traffic so they were not ever stopped but their speed was not near the limit.

The traffic really jammed up on them as they took Exit 1B toward the stadium.

"It's like this every night they play. Even when they're losing," Gene sounded puzzled.

"Yeah, I probably shoulda cut through town but I didn't want to fight the lights."

"Did you call ahead?"

"I asked Thor to let park security know we were coming. That's all. I don't want them trying to stop Demming. That's our job."

"Well, we need to get there first."

"Hang on, I'm taking the shoulder." At this, Ron pulled far to the left and touched his siren again. Cars that were moving slowly began to inch to the right and he maneuvered his Sentra onto the left shoulder with less than six inches to spare. Cars began to honk and drivers further ahead saw what was happening and began their rightward inching well ahead of the arrival of Looney's car. Even so, it took them more than four minutes to make the half-mile to Exit 1B where the cars were leaving the Interstate for the ballpark.

Ron continued his move on the left shoulder through the exit and down onto Second Street but then faced three lanes of traffic between him and the right turn on Nuxhall to get to the park. Fortunately, he had several blocks to travel before the turn was needed and he used that to weave into any opening to his right using the lights and the siren liberally.

"You're not gonna find a parking place," Gene noted wisely as they headed for the intersection.

"Not even thinking about it, "Ron said wheeling off Second Street onto Nuxhall and making a wide U-turn to park on the side of the road next to the park. He unbuckled and reached under the seat for a placard reading "POLICE" that he placed on the dash as he got out. Gene joined him and they jogged to the Home Plate entrance to the park.

There were lines of people at the entrances and the shortest was the line marked 'Season ticket Holders" so they pushed in that direction. Ron did not join the line but signaled the security man at the metal detector that he wanted to talk.

"Not now buddy, we working here."

Ron flashed his badge and said, "Now."

The man approached somewhat sullenly, "You want free entrance, officer?"

"I want more than that," Ron snapped. "I want your supervisor, here. Now."

The man, large but mostly stomach, stepped back and said, "What?"

"We called Security to say we were coming ten minutes ago. Check with your supervisor. And we're coming in."

Looney and Gene both slid past the metal detector flashing badges and weapons at the security man. He punched a button on his walkie-talkie and began to talk rapidly. Within 20 seconds there was a flurry of red-jacketed men moving quickly across the area behind the detector and one of them with three badges around his neck and the most gray in his hair came to Ron.

'Are you the detectives?"

"Yes. We need to get to Section 302 as quickly as possible."

"Follow me," the leader said and moved at a brisk jaunt toward the stands. No one looked at the guard who frowned, looked around, and shrugged before resuming his position at the metal detector.

The security man led them to the beginning of the stand structure and indicated the ramp or the elevator with a question on his face. Gene quickly moved to the elevator and pushed the up button. He stepped back and waited. Nothing seemed to happen for over a minute and then he thought he could hear the motor of the elevator. After a few seconds, the sound stopped, and finally, the door opened. Looney and Gene pushed toward the opening and were met by a wall of humanity exiting the elevator. They pushed their way through and determined that the 300 level suites would be accessed on the third floor. The elevator doors started to slowly close and Ron thought they acted more than a little like his knees did on cold mornings, stiff and slow. Just before the door closed, a hand jutted into the opening and triggered the doors to slowly retract into the open position again. This allowed the man who had inserted his hand and about twelve other people to enter the elevator.

There was some shoving and good-natured ribbing in the group as some were wearing Reds gear and others were wearing Pittsburgh hats. During the jostling to get everyone situated, someone pushed the button for Level Two.

By the time they were able to leave the elevator on Level Three, Ron and Gene were way behind their schedule. Fortunately, Section 302 was a short distance away. Unfortunately, it was behind another set of guarded doors. The security people at this entrance looked more attentive to their job and Ron went to the one on the right side expecting a discussion and some supervisory contact. As he pulled his badge, the guard said, "Detective?"

"Right."

"Let me show you where Section 302 is." The guard nodded to his partner and led the detectives through the door and down a carpeted hallway to a lounge area with a bar and two food kiosks. He indicated where the lounge opened to the playing field; the glass door was labeled "#301-#302."

Ron patted the security guard on the arm and asked him to remain where he was. Then he and Gene went through the door into the seating area and quickly began looking for the Dean.

When he didn't immediately see her, Ron moved down the steps to the front of the section and looked back into the faces of the scattered fans seated in Section 302. He still did not see her. There were several empty seats due to the spacing policy for live attendance at games and he thought perhaps she had not arrived yet. He caught Gene's eye and shrugged. They met at the bottom of the stairs.

"Now what?" Gene asked. "I don't want to comb this entire place."

"Shouldn't have to. She's got club tickets and that means free food. If she's not here maybe she's inside the club."

They started their way back up the stairs and the usher for the section stopped them. "Are you looking for someone in particular?" she asked.

"Yes," Looney said. "Dean Wisener."

"Uh, His name's not Dean. I think it's Robert; he's right there." She pointed to an average-looking man sitting in the middle of the section. By himself.

CHAPTER 58

Friday, April 15

The usher was pleased to introduce Ron to Mr. Robert Wisener, whom she knew only by his first name.

"Robert, this man is looking for you."

"Really? Hello, what can I do for you?"

"Sir, I am Detective Ron Looney of the Homicide Division. I spoke with your wife earlier."

"Today?"

"No, sir. Earlier, at the medical school."

"What about? You did say Homicide, didn't you?"

"Yes, sir. We need to find her. Can you tell me where she is?"

"Well, she's not here, right now, but she'll be back soon."

"Sir, where is your wife?"

"See here, detective. What is this all about? Why do you need to see her this very minute?"

Ron slid into the row of seats and sat next to the Dean's husband. He lowered his voice and turned to face the playing field so that others might not be able to hear his words.

"Sir, your wife is in danger, and we need to find her right away."

Robert Wisener had to lean forward to hear Ron, but he did not lower his voice, "Danger? What do you mean?"

"Please keep your voice down, sir. I have reason to believe that a man intends to attack her here at the ballpark…"

Robert started to rise, saying, "What? Let's go get her…"

Ron pulled his arm and got him reseated. "We will get her, sir. Where is she?"

"She, uh, she went to get something to eat."

"In the club?"

"Ah, no, it's outside the club."

Ron wanted to roll his eyes at the circumspect answers he got. Instead, he put his hand on Robert's arm and squeezed until the man looked him in the eyes. Then he said, "We have police in the park, and we will take care of this if you will just tell me where she went." His voice was tempered and modulated but punched out the last three words.

Robert sat very still and swallowed. His voice was low and broken, "I don't really know."

"What was she going to get?'

"Funnel cake, I think."

"Where is the funnel cake sold?"

"I don't know. I've never gotten it here."

Ron signaled to the usher. She leaned over, and he asked, "Where is funnel cake sold in the park?"

"I, uh, I don't know. I only work here in the club."

Gene had listened to the conversation from the lower row, and he moved out and went to the Security guard.

"Where do they sell funnel cake in the park?"

"What's funnel cake?"

"You know, that pastry pushed out of a funnel into boiling oil and covered in powdered sugar."

"Oh, the strudel."

"Whatever, where do I get it?'

"I think it's down on the main level."

Ron joined his partner, "Is there only one place selling it?"

"I think so," the guard answered, sensing their anxiety.

Ron turned to the usher and said, "You stay here with the husband and help this man," he indicated the guard, "protect Dean Wisener if she comes back here." Turning to the guard, he instructed, "Here's my card with my cell phone number. If she gets back here, you keep everyone away from her and call me immediately, Got that?" He was moving away even before the man started nodding.

Gene followed him up the short set of stairs to re-enter the club, and they started for the elevator area. Pushing their way through some individuals entering the club and passing the identification check-point, Ron saw a sign indicating a stairwell and directed them toward it.

He pulled the door open and was greeted by a string of young men and women in red blazers filling the stairwell and exiting on the third level. He and Gene struggled to get into the stairwell, let alone try to descend until the crowd cleared. They raced down the steps two at a time and came out on the main level. They both stopped and looked in each direction, realizing they were on a circular concourse and they had no idea which way to go to get to the funnel cake kiosk.

After a moment, Ron spied another security guard, and this one knew exactly where the kiosk was. He pointed them in the right direction and said, "It's right around section 110, I think."

They thanked him and started in that direction, checking the overhead signs that indicated they were at section 122. They were also at the Home Plate Gate and facing crowds of people swarming into the park. These people were moving in both directions, with them and against them. A considerable number stood still, looking at their ticket and trying to determine where their seats were. The moving stream of people parted around them like a stream avoids boulders. The effect was to strand and separate the detectives at first. They moved quickly through the crowd, however, bobbing and weaving. They met up shoulder to shoulder in a crowd of slow walking people as they got to section 117.

The larger, permanent food and drink counters were on the outside of the concourse. That left the smaller, individual kiosks to be placed closer to the playing field. Ron knew that's where they would find the funnel cakes. As they neared section 110, they slowed as much as possible without being pushed from behind and searched the area for signs.

Ron suddenly pointed at a man and said to Gene, "Ask him."

Gene noted the man was carrying a paper plate with a steaming pastry covered in powdered sugar.

"Excuse me, sir, where did you get that?"

"Uh, you mean the funnel cake?"

"Yes."

"Right back there," he said, nodding toward a kiosk that was facing the playing field and not the concourse.

"Thanks," Gene said and signaled to Ron. They moved toward the area and saw a line of maybe a dozen individuals. When they were about twenty-five feet away, Gene grabbed Ron's sleeve and stopped.

He motioned with his head toward the front end of the line. Both of them became acutely aware of Dean Wisener about to place her order, leaning over the glass case around the cooking oil.

Before they could relax, however, a movement at the cashier's position caught their eye. Terry Demming was standing just a step away from the cashier, eyes fixed on the Dean with only two people between him and her. Terry's right arm extended down at his side. In his hand, he held a small object that glinted in the light.

CHAPTER 59

Friday, April 15

Gene tensed as he recognized Demming. He felt Ron's grip on his arm tighten, as well. The young man was casually dressed in slacks and a sweatshirt with a hood. He appeared uneasy, turning his head to check the surroundings when Ron saw and recognized him. Otherwise, he appeared very unremarkable in the khakis and grey top. The detectives realized that Demming had no idea who they were. Gene noted other signs of nervousness as Demming's right foot was repeatedly tapping the ground. He also kept flexing his left hand. Gene glanced at Ron and nodded, then moved to his left toward Demming's rear. Ron went to his right and joined the line of funnel cake buyers. But he didn't stop at the end of the line. He created some commotion by pushing through the gathering and ducking under the restraining tape to where the line joined the kiosk.

That was where Janet Wisener stood giving her order to the cook. Ron slipped under the tape and loudly noted, "Well, Janet, I thought you would have gotten your order by now."

She turned surprised, but before she could speak, Ron moved between her and where Demming was waiting, placing his body in the way of Demming seeing her face. He spoke again, clearly too loudly for the closeness, "Yes, I know I said I'd wait upstairs, but I decided to join you." Some of the grumblings behind him faded away.

She tried to speak, "Detectiv …"

"Detecting that the funnel cake was exactly what we needed for dessert. You are right!"

"I don't' under…"

"I just decided to join you. Isn't that a good thing?" Ron was trying to get her to play along with him, but she was looking for some reason for him to have jumped into line with her.

"Perhaps we should get two cakes, "Ron said, turning to look at the cook. He saw out of the side of his visual field that the person just ahead of Dean Wisener had paid for his cake and was moving away, leaving the space at the register open.

"I don't…" the Dean tried again.

" Well, maybe one will do, then," Ron said, pulling out his wallet and moving as if to make a payment. The cook handed a fresh funnel cake to the cashier, who began to dust it with powdered sugar. The Dean looked from Ron to the person with the sugar and raised her shoulders in perplexity.

Ron shifted again to maintain his position between the Dean and the killer poised just past the register. He could see Demming's plan in his mind's eye: the Dean would turn from the register and be facing Demming. His slash would be quick and likely not noticed by many in the crowd. As the Dean would begin to fall to the ground, Demming would yell something like 'Get her some help!' and then fade into the crowd and disappear. Ron was not going to let that happen. He was between the Dean and Demming.

The cashier handed the powdered cake over the counter to the Dean. She accepted it with both hands and looked questioningly at Ron. He was reluctant to take it from her and encumber his hands in any ensuing scuffle. He shook his head and nodded briefly that she should hold the plate, and they started to turn toward where Demming was standing. Ron pivoted to keep himself between her and the coming attack.

Just then, a loud voice with a touch of western twang rang out, "Well, I'll be … It's ole Terry Demming! Hey, Terry, I almost didn't recognize you."

Ron saw Demming stiffen and reflexively turn toward his rear to see who was calling him. His turn was interrupted. Gene hit him in the nose with a strong left jab when he was halfway around. Demming stumbled back a half pace and started to react, but before he could do so, Ron pushed him in the back toward Gene.

Gene completed the scenario with a solid right cross that hit Demming on the point of his jaw and just a little to his left. Demming's head spun rapidly up and to his right just before his eyes glazed, and he crumpled down to the ground. The events occurred rapidly enough that many bystanders did not actually see the blows. Those who did pushed themselves back away from the scene; only one pulled out a phone.

Ron bent over the prostrate man and held out his hand to Gene, who passed him handcuffs. Gene also pulled his badge and showed it to the gathered crowd, "Nothing to see here, folks. Routine police matter. Please go on about your business." And a few of them did; most, however, stood rooted to the spot and watched.

Once Ron had secured Demming's hands, he pulled out his phone and called for backup and transport. Then he stood and clapped Gene on the shoulder, "How long since you've had that kind of set-up?"

"Never. In all my fights, it was just me in the ring with the other guy. Never had anyone to knock him off his balance so I could get that cross in."

"Well, it sure looked pretty from the rear."

Ron turned to the Dean was standing wide-eyed behind him.

"Ma'am, I'm sorry I had to jump out at you like that. I didn't want him getting close to you."

"Is that …?"

"Yes, ma'am. He's the one that's been killing those others."

"That's Dr. Schlecter?"

"Oh, no. ma'am. We figured out a couple of days back that this guy, Terry Demming, was the killer. He set Schlecter up as a decoy. I can explain all this to you later."

"Later… Yes, that would be good."

"Say, why don't you just take that funnel cake back to your seat and enjoy the game. Robert is worried about you."

"Robert, yes."

By this time, two additional CPD uniforms had arrived, and a couple of park security officers. Ron asked one of the security men to escort the Dean to her seat and explain things to her husband. The Dean left, still a bit wide-eyed but able to say, "Thank you," both to Ron and Gene.

Ron pulled a groggy Demming to his feet and gave the uniforms responsibility for taking him to the station for booking. Before they left, Gene went to the area where Demming had been lying on the ground and picked up a plastic-handle surgical knife using a tissue. He put it in a plastic envelope and gave it to the uniforms as evidence.

People were getting back in line and paying little attention to the two detectives. Gene turned back toward his partner. Silently they bumped fists and headed for their car.

CHAPTER 60

Thursday, April 21

Tom had opened the drapes in his office to let the spring sunshine in and lighten the room. The mood of the three men in the room was also light and upbeat. Tom sat, as usual, behind his desk. Ron Looney sat in a wingback over-stuffed chair near the window, and Gene perched in a wooden straight chair to the right side of Tom's desk. Each man had a recently brewed cup of coffee from the Green Bean kiosk in the lobby. Nick, the barista, had created each of the drinks with a flair and pizzazz as if he knew the men were celebrating.

Tom tipped his drink toward each of the others and said, "I really don't want to ever go through this again."

"No need, General," Ron said, solemnly. "Just don't hire any more murderers, and you'll do just fine, I reckon."

Gene snickered and covered his laugh by sipping on his drink.

"You're not going to get this around to being my fault, Master Sergeant, no matter how hard you try," Tom answered.

"Well, we'll just have to see how the future goes. Right, Gene?"

"We sure have had a lot of business here at New City," Gene said slowly." Not that I'm complaining. I mean, if we have to go somewhere to tie up crime, I'd just as soon do it here with one of Nick's 'usuals'."

"Speaking of tying things up, didn't you promise me a complete story?" Tom asked, looking at Looney.

"Yes. Yes, I did. Demming is spilling the story, and it's mostly complete and rather like we had put it together."

Gene added, "As we finally put it together."

Ron stared at his partner. "Still …"

Gene decided to pick up the storyline. "Demming was an average kid with average grades who wanted to go to medical school. Any number of people advised him, and apparently, no one would say, 'Give it up, guy. That's not a reasonable goal for you.' They kept telling him there was some possibility if he would do just a little bit more, or do something different."

Ron jumped back in. "Or do it some other place. When he couldn't get into the medical schools near his home in Nevada, he came to Ohio to establish residency, intending to apply to every school in the state.

"He started in Akron at one of the newest schools. Even got a job at the primary teaching hospital, Akron General. But, advisors there recognized his poor scholastic work in college. They recommended he seek a Master's degree to show his capability for academic work. I suspect they thought he would either have significant trouble enrolling or completing such a rigorous course."

Tom asked, "Was that why he ended up in Cincinnati?"

"Yes," Ron replied, "as best as we can determine. His roommate in Akron said he looked around in various places to find a Masters and the one he settled on was here at Cincy State."

"You think that was because programs in Cleveland and Columbus turned him down."

"I do, but let me be clear. I do not have any evidence of that. He did get accepted into the medical informatics program here at Cincy State. Once he got here, he pursued admission to South West Ohio Medical School. He ran into Dr. Finkbeiner at some gym and heard that working at New City in the research program would be better than an informatics degree, and he dropped out. He then came here to the hospital and met with Piringa, who recommended he work with Schlecter. Said Schlecter was doing important, high impact research. Told him he could get an online degree in Anatomy or something at the same time. That was never going to be a real option for this kid."

"What caused the derailment?" Tom asked.

"Apparently, he got his letter of denial to SWOMS the same day he lost his job and the opportunity to coat-tail on Schlecter. And he went ballistic. All the failures and dropped opportunities built up, and he decided to take it out on Schlecter. He was waiting for him when he went by the lab to get things before going on sabbatical.

"Demming made Schlecter drive out to that construction site where he had left his own car. He said he did not plan to kill him, but Schlecter was so despondent and enervated he didn't fight back. Demming said Schlecter kept saying, 'My fault' and things like that. So he kept hitting him with fists, rocks, and finally a big stick. When he realized he was dead, he tried to hide the body. Apparently, his billfold fell out of his shirt pocket during this without him being aware."

Gene added in the small silence, "He decided to keep the Mercedes. When he heard from the news that Schlecter was a 'person of interest', he knew he couldn't use the car to get around. He parked it in the hospital parking deck and moved it every couple of days. It was muddy and dirty from the construction site, and the license was not readable. He ate and slept in the car and used it to attack the others."

"Everything fell apart when he failed to kill Dr. Escobar," Ron added. He decided to end everything by killing Dean Wisener and then disappearing. He thought we were still looking for Schlecter and probably considering him to be dead."

Gene said, "He actually called the Dean's office and got her schedule for going to the ball game. What guts."

Tom nodded and grinned, "I also understand you used some college tricks to catch him."

Ron laughed, "Well, Gene was a champion boxer in college. I finally got to see what he's been hiding."

"Not hiding, partner. Kept in reserve, if you will. Possibly classified as deadly weapons."

"It was pretty deadly for Demming."

Tom asked, "How did you do it?"

"Gene cold-cocked him. Got him to turn around and Bif! Bam! There he was lying on the ground. And he hasn't been a bit of trouble since."

Tom saluted them both with his cup again. "You know, I think we should have a boxing team here at the hospital, Gene. There are some people here causing me trouble. You want to join the team?"

<u>ACKNOWLEDGEMENTS</u>

I want to thank my wife and children for their encouragement during this writing process. Their feedback, support, and encouragement were positive factors in me finishing the original manuscript.

I also want to recognize Elle Murray for her faithful and frequent efforts to clean up the manuscript and to assist me in getting to the right place in decisions about format, artistry, and pagination.

Any errors that escaped these screening activities are mine alone.

Galen Barbour
Alexandria, Virginia
January 2023

Want more medical murder mystery?
Turn the page for an excerpt from the next book in the Ron
Looney series

A dead man is found in a storage room in New City hospital. The
man is naked and is not known to the employees. Tom Bolling, chief
of staff, asks his friend, Ron Looney to assist in unraveling the mystery
of the death and identification. Ron and his partner, Gene Novalchek,
soon find themselves wrestling with corporate greed and attempted
murder as well.

As usual, this soon after quitting time, the bar was not yet full. Two of the customers were at the bar when the man entered, and they paid him little attention. They were sitting two stools apart, socially distanced and occupied with their own thoughts; one reading the sports page, the other looking at his phone. At the rear, on the right, a gray haired couple sat in a booth across from each other. One of the pool tables was occupied; a pair of roughnecks in checkered flannel shirts was playing for money. The jukebox was playing softly and the only person to notice the man's entrance was the barmaid.

He was dressed differently from the bar's usual patrons. They wore denim pants with flannel shirts; he was wearing a suit. Most of them were hefty men, and he was thin. He seemed clearly out of his element in the bar and stood just inside the door and looked around uncertainly before cautiously moving to the bar. He was reminded of the protagonist's entrance in the Shooting of Dan McGrew "fresh from the creeks and loaded for bear'. Except that he didn't feel 'loaded for bear'.

The woman behind the bar glanced up and smiled, "Whatcha have, honey?"

"Uh, maybe a beer?"

"Draft or bottle?"

"Draft, I guess."

"Good call," she said and reached for a mug. The man in the suit looked around the bar noting empty booths and stools and smiled nervously at her.

"You looking for somebody, honey?" she asked while pulling his beer.

"Ah, yes. To meet here. I, ah, appear to be early."

"Well, take your beer and go sit in that booth right there," she said motioning to the left side of the establishment. "You can see anybody who comes in."

"Thanks," he said, carefully picking up the filled mug and carrying it with both hands like it might contain explosives. He looked at the booth and placed himself in the back corner where he could watch the door. He found a coaster that read, "Friends don't let Friends go Thirsty" in a small holder at the back of the booth. He put his beer on the coaster and rubbed his hands on his pants. The barmaid went back to her work.

The man sat in the booth and looked at the mug in front of him for a few minutes. He looked up every time the door opened with fading hope in his eyes. At last, he lifted the mug with both hands and took a deep sip of the golden liquid. As he sat the mug down, he realized he had gotten suds on his nose and began searching his pockets for his handkerchief. He found it, wiped his nose, and then decided to clean his glasses as well.

A moment later, he looked up to find a man standing beside the booth holding a mug of beer. This man was of a size like others in the bar. He wore heavy khaki pants, work boots, and a long-sleeve denim shirt.

"Oh, hey," the man in the booth said. "I didn't see you …"

"No names, okay?" the other man said, as he sat down across from the man in the suit. "Never know who might be listening. No proper nouns."

The man in the suit thought for a brief second and then nodded his agreement. "Are we in trouble?"

"I don't think so, but let's not start anything. You can never tell who is listening to a conversation in a bar."

"All right." The suit took another two-handed sip of beer, this time avoiding the foam on the nose.

"I just think we should agree on what we have found so far," said the newcomer, sipping from his drink as well.

"Okay."

"I told you that number you gave me didn't work and there's no website either."

"Yes, I remember. I checked the number against the invoice. It's accurate. But I also found there's no street address on the invoice either."

"Now that's really strange, right?" The larger man lifted his mug and drank. "You said you found something else that's odd?"

"Well, I also found some additional invoices from, ah, that company for some other jobs, too."

"What do you mean, 'other jobs'?"

"Other than the one we were initially talking about."

"So, this isn't the only time!"

"It seems so. There were several other jobs. Over several years. And that's not the only odd thing about it."

"Really? This is getting deep."

The man in the suit seemed uneasy about that remark and looked over his shoulder and around the bar before adding, "All the invoices are for the exact same dollar amount. Every time, every month, no matter what the job."

"All right, now. That is very suspicious. Who are these guys?"

The man in the suit eyed the surroundings again and leaned across the table to whisper, " I think I know."

"Tell me."

"I looked the company up in Zippia to see …"

"What's that?"

"A listing of jobs. Anyway, the company is listed but without contact information. And they aren't advertising for workers, either. So, I called a friend at Dun and Bradstreet. There is no listing for that company!"

"And that's important, why?"

"If a company isn't listed with Dun and Bradstreet, it means it doesn't really do business and has no credit history."

"Wait a minute. You're saying these guys aren't even real? If that's true you have turned over a big rock."

The man in the suit sat up a little straighter and said, "That's not all. It would be hard for them to operate here in Ohio without some cover. So, I called the Secretary of State in Columbus."

"Should I know what that was about?"

"I don't know. The reason I called was to determine whether the … uh, company, was operating legally."

"Okay, then. What did you find?"

"I got the incorporation information."

The larger man said, "I wouldn't have thought of that. What'd those documents show?"

The man sat up straighter in his seat, leaned forward and spoke softly, "Three incorporators. A lawyer, now retired, a woman, and a man.

"Okay. I don't know what that means."

"Well, the man turns out to be her son."

"Tight group."

"Yeah. Wait till you hear who her husband is."